Alice & Megan's
COOKBOOK

MEGAN SHEEHAN lives in Limerick with her parents, her sister Rosie and her cat, Domino. When she grows up, she'd like to work with animals.

ALICE O'ROURKE has one little brother, Jamie. She generously divides her time between her mum's flat and her dad's house. When she grows up, she'd like to work with humans.

JUDI CURTIN grew up in Cork and now lives in Limerick where she is married with three children. Her seven bestselling 'Alice & Megan' books, and *Eva's Journey*, are published by The O'Brien Press. With Roisin Meaney, she is the author of *See If I Care*, and she has also written three novels, *Sorry, Walter*, *From Claire to Here* and *Almost Perfect*. Her books have been translated into Serbian, Portuguese and German.

The 'Alice & Megan' series
Alice Next Door
Alice Again
Don't Ask Alice
Alice in the Middle
Bonjour Alice
Alice & Megan Forever
Alice to the Rescue

Praise for the 'Alice & Megan' series
'If you like Jacqueline Wilson, then you'll love Judi Curtin!'
Primary Times

'Rising star Judi Curtin's "Alice" books celebrate friendship, humour and loyalty.' *Sunday Independent*

Judi Curtin

Alice & Megan's
COOKBOOK

Illustrated by
Woody Fox

THE O'BRIEN PRESS
DUBLIN

First published 2010 by The O'Brien Press Ltd,
12 Terenure Road East, Rathgar, Dublin 6, Ireland.
Tel: +353 1 4923333; Fax: +353 1 4922777
E-mail: books@obrien.ie; Website: www.obrien.ie

ISBN: 978-1-84717-215-0
A catalogue record for this title is available from the British Library
1 2 3 4 5 6 7 8
10 11 12 13 14 15
The O'Brien Press receives
assistance from

Illustrations: Woody Fox
Layout and design: The O'Brien Press Ltd
Printed and bound in Poland by
Białostockie Zakłady Graficzne S.A.
The paper in this book is produced
using pulp from managed forests.

Dedication

For Mum and Dad who taught me to cook – who'd have thought it would come to this!

Acknowledgements

Huge thanks to everyone who helped with this book.

Thanks to Dan and Brian for bravely eating whatever was put in front of them as I tested recipes. Thanks to Ellen and Annie for doing some of the testing for me when I couldn't face the kitchen any more.

Lots of people gave me ideas for recipes. Cooking ideas go back and forth a lot in my family, and lest I offend anyone, thanks to Mum, Dad, Mary, Derek, Declan, Eileen, Caroline, Martin, Kieran and Kim. Thanks to Sarah and Alison for the sausage rolls. Thanks to Liz for 'Melissa's Chicken'. Thanks to Ellen for the warm salad. Thanks to Jane for the yummy dip. Thanks to Elaine for the chocolate biscuit cake. Thanks to Mary for sharing her extensive library.

Big apologies if I've been cooking your signature dish for so long that I've forgotten the source – consider yourself thanked in spirit.

Thanks to Woody for still more great illustrations.

Thanks, as always, to everyone at The O'Brien Press. Thanks to Michael, for not laughing when I said 'Let's do a cookbook.' Thanks to Emma for beautiful design work. Thanks to my editor, Helen, who kept me going as it slowly dawned on me how hard it is to actually write a cookbook.

Contents:

Why We Wrote This Cookbook
By Megan Sheehan

Welcome to *Alice & Megan's Cookbook*. You may ask how we came to write it, when everyone knows Alice is the world's worst cook—

I am not, Miss Leonard said I had a very original approach to Home Ec. – Alice

Well, if you want to take that as a compliment, Alice …
Anyway, maybe the easiest way to explain how it happened would be to let you take a peek into my SECRET diary …

Megan's Top Secret Diary.
Keep out! (You too, Alice!)

Monday

We had a big assembly at school today. Our principal, Mrs Kingston, said that all first years have to do a big project. I got very nervous when I heard that. It reminded me of the time she announced the essay competition that nearly ended up with Alice going to France for four whole months.

Anyway, this new project isn't anything like that. Everyone has to come up with an idea to raise money for the construction of a new school hockey pitch.

Joe asked if there was a prize for whoever makes the most money. Mrs Kingston gave him an evil look, and said,

'Yes, Joe, there is a prize, and the prize is the sense of satisfaction in having raised the most money for a good cause.'

Everyone (except Joe) thought that was really funny.

I've been thinking about the project all evening, and I have a totally brilliant idea. I'm going to take twelve photos of Domino, and put them together to make a calendar. For the August photo, I'm going to make her sit in a sand-bucket, and for December, I'm going to make her wear a Santa hat. She's going to be sooo cute that no one will be able to resist buying the calendar.

Alice texted me a while ago, and said that for her project she's going to make and sell a cookbook.

That girl can be sooooo funny sometimes.

Tuesday

Alice wasn't joking!!!!

'Don't you love my cookery book idea?' she asked me on the way to school this morning.

'But ......' I began.

Is there a polite way to say – you're a total disaster in the kitchen?

As usual, Alice was able to read my mind.

'I know I'm not exactly the best cook in the world,' she said. 'But that's why I'm the perfect person to write a cookbook. I know how many things can go wrong.'

What she said did have a weird kind of logic, but it's still a crazy idea.

Hundreds of people could be poisoned.

Alice can't be allowed to write a cookbook!

I'm going to have to figure out a way to make her change her mind.

Wednesday

When did I ever manage to change Alice's mind about anything?

She's determined to write a recipe book, and in the interest of public health, I can't allow her to do it on her own.

Can't she remember the disastrous queen cakes she made that were rejected by a starving stray dog??

Has she managed to forget how the whole school had to be evacuated when her Madeira cake set off the smoke alarms????

Alice isn't sure how to make a chicken sandwich but she wants to write a recipe for Tamarind Marinated Chicken Breast in Coconut Chickpea Flour Curry!!!!

Served with Barley and Wild Rice Pilaf with Pomegranate Seeds!!!!!!!!!!

So I've had to come to a difficult decision. Poor little Domino is never going to be the star of her own personal calendar.

I'm going to have to help Alice with her cookbook. I know lots of recipes. Mum will tell me how to make some of her favourite dishes (and if she promises to cut back on the lentils, I might even use some of them). Rosie is good at cooking too, and she'd love to be part of a book. We can ask Grace and Louise and Kellie for ideas too.

Alice and Megan's recipe book is on its way!

Writing it is going to be great fun I think!

Tips for Cooking Success

Cooking is great fun, and when you make stuff yourself it always tastes better.

Don't panic though if things don't turn out perfectly the first time – everything improves with practice. LEARN FROM YOUR MISTAKES.

Before you start, read the recipe right to the end, and take out all your ingredients. (You don't want to fire ahead and find that the last ingredient is Monrovian crimble-berry juice and you're all out of it!)

Make sure you have all the tools and utensils that you are going to need.

Oven temperatures vary. We've used an electric fan oven and a gas oven. If you have an electric oven that's not fan-assisted, you might need to cook at a slightly higher temperature. (Temperature Coversions, p152)

When baking, resist the urge to open the oven before it's time to check if your cake is done. Opening the oven door too soon can make your cakes end up like the Titanic – sunk!

We've used a 'difficulty rating' on our recipes in this book – one wooden spoon for the easiest up to three for the hardest. But with a bit of practice you'll soon be cooking them all!

Health & Safety
By Megan

Writing a cookbook is a big responsibility, so I asked my mum and Miss Leonard for some advice on health and safety. This is what they told me:

Safety in the Kitchen:

Kitchens can be dangerous places, and hospitals aren't all that much fun, Don't remind me! – Alice so remember to follow a few simple safety rules.

1. If you aren't used to cooking, it's best to cook while there's an adult within shouting distance. If you're not sure about anything, ask the adult.

Veronica doesn't spend much time in the kitchen, so if she's the only adult around, maybe you should telephone someone like Sheila for advice! – Alice

2. You can't cook a whole lot without using knives, but always be careful with them. Never use a knife with the blade pointing towards you, and always pay attention to what

you are doing. Bits of your fingers aren't going to improve the taste of what you are cooking!

3. Be careful around the cooker. Keep the handles of pots and pans turned to the side, so you don't bump into them and knock them over. Use an oven glove to carry hot plates and pans. Be extra careful with gas hobs. Ask an adult to help if you're not sure how to use it. Never lean across an open flame, and make sure that you don't have dangly string or ribbons on your clothes that could catch fire. Steam can burn too, so be careful!

4. Keep pets out of the kitchen. Domino makes the sweetest paw-prints ever, but even I don't like seeing them on top of freshly-iced chocolate cakes. There's also a danger of tripping over pets if they get underfoot, or they could be splashed with something hot.

5. If you're using an electric beater or a blender for the first time, ask an adult to help. Keep fingers and hair clear of blades and whisks. Turn off the power when you're finished and don't try to remove lids while parts are still moving — unless you fancy redecorating your kitchen.

Hygiene

If you are cooking for friends, you (probably) don't want to poison them, so follow some simple rules.

1. Wash your hands before you start, and make sure that surfaces and utensils are clean.

2. If you have long hair, tie it back. Your hair might be pretty, but your friends are sooo not going to want to eat it. Hair in food is just gross.

3. Wear an apron. It might make you look like your granny, but if your friends call unexpectedly, you don't want your clothes to be covered it half-cooked food. Do you??

4. If you have had fun, be sure to clean up the kitchen after you. You want to be allowed to cook again next time, don't you?

Food Safety

If you don't cook food properly, there can be some very ugly results. So even if you're hosting a dinner party for all your favourite people in the whole world i.e.: Melissa, Hazel, Miss Leonard and Mrs O'Callaghan, you need to follow some rules. Must we? – Alice

1. Eggs are delicious, but raw eggs can sometimes have a gross bug called 'salmonella', which can be dangerous, especially for babies, sick people and old people, so to be on the safe side (where my mum always stands!) cook all eggs thoroughly before serving.

2. You also need to be careful with chicken. Never, ever chop raw chicken or any raw meat on the same chopping board as other ingredients. Knives, chopping boards and hands that have been near chicken need to be washed well in hot soapy water. Never use the same utensils for chicken and food that is to be served raw. Always check that chicken is well cooked before serving. There can't be any pink left at all. If in doubt, ask an adult, or cook for another while.

3. Red meats, like beef and lamb, need to be brown on the outside before serving. With these meats, pink on the inside is OK, but only if the meat isn't minced. Anything with minced meat — like burgers or meatballs — must be cooked until there is no pink left.

4. Never store raw and cooked meat together in the fridge; make sure they are in separate containers or wrappings.

5. Chillies can give great zing to a dish, but be careful. Put in too many and it won't be very nice. The hottest parts of a chilli are the seeds, and the white membrane inside. Leave these out unless you are a complete heat-freak. Always wash your hands well after handling chillies — be very careful not to touch your eyes before washing your hands — that's *so* not funny!

 **Ingredients
By Alice & Megan**

A Note from Miss Leonard on Substituting Ingredients:
Rules are rules, and recipes are for following, not messing around with.

A Note from Alice on Substituting Ingredients:
Where's the fun in that? What does Miss Leonard know anyway?

Er, she's a Home Ec. teacher! — Megan

Whatever. Cooking should be fun. — Alice

A Note from Megan on Substituting Ingredients:
I understand what Alice is saying — sort of. Experimenting with ingredients can be fun, but don't just fling any old thing in.

A Note from Sheila on Substituting Ingredients:
Wasting food is very wrong, so when experimenting, remember that (unless it's poisonous) you're going to have to eat it!

Eggs: When we say 'eggs', we mean hens' eggs. If you have ducks running around your garden, their eggs can be used for most of our recipes. Quails' eggs, while totally cute, are not really suitable for the recipes in this book. Or for any recipes in my Home Ec. class — Miss Leonard

Vegetables: If you totally hate a particular vegetable, you can usually swap it for something else.

Sprouts — Alice
Broccoli — Megan

However, tomatoes and onions are often essential to a recipe, and your dish might taste a bit strange without them.

Herbs

Because we practised most of these recipes in Megan's house, we had a whole garden full of fresh herbs to choose from. Not everyone can grow herbs Why not? Hasn't everyone got a window-sill? — Sheila so you can use dried herbs instead. Just remember that dried herbs taste stronger than fresh ones, so you'll need to use a bit less.

Fish

Fish is very good for you, and you can help to make it good for the environment too. Some fish is endangered and it's best not to add to that problem. When you're buying fish, ask the seller if it's ocean-friendly — it's their job to know that kind of stuff!

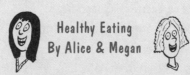

Healthy Eating
By Alice & Megan

Sheila said that if we write something about healthy food, she'll persuade all the members of her allotment gardening club to buy a copy of this book (and we need all the sales we can get), so here goes.

Sheila said that we should say that your body is like an engine, and if you don't give it the right fuel, you can't expect it to work properly.

Once my mum put the wrong fuel into her car — petrol instead of diesel. I don't know if it damaged the engine, but it sure damaged my ears. The language my mum used soooo wasn't suitable for a thirteen-year-old to hear. — Alice

Sheila said that we should also tell you about the food pyramid. You probably know about that already (teachers love giving lessons on the food pyramid). And besides, it's a bit too complicated for us to explain (Ok, so we admit we weren't listening when Miss Leonard talked about it).

Anyway, the basic message is that some food is really good for you, and some isn't. (Big surprise) You should eat lots of the good foods – that's fruit, vegetables, brown rice, potatoes … *Don't forget porridge! – Sheila*

You shouldn't eat so much of the foods that aren't so good for you – that's sweets, cakes, chocolate. *They're all my favourites – Jamie* It's best just to eat small portions of these, or save them for special occasions.

Tips & Techniques By Megan

Melting Chocolate

Lots of our recipes use melted chocolate and it's important to do this properly. First you need to put some water into a small saucepan and put it on to simmer. Then you need to find a very clean and dry bowl that can sit on the saucepan without touching the water. Break up your chocolate, put into the bowl, and allow it to melt, stirring around occasionally. If the chocolate gets wet, it turns horribly dull and grainy, so watch out for this. (In 'Rosie's Favourite Chocolate Cake' the recipe asks you to add water with butter, and in that case, that's OK!) You can also melt butter using this method.

'Softened Butter'

This is just regular butter left out of the fridge for about half an hour to soften.

'Rubbing In'

You often need to 'rub in' ingredients. This is exactly as it sounds. You just rub the ingredients between your fingers until they look like very fine breadcrumbs, with no big lumps.

Key:
Easy peasy-
A little bit harder-
You can do it-
(but don't be afraid to ask for help if you need it!)

Alice's Recipes   Sheila's Recipes
Megan's Recipes   Melissa's Recipes

HAVE FUN!

Brilliant Breakfasts

Bananas & Yoghurt

Everyone knows that my mum thinks that porridge is the best breakfast in the world. But even saints have their off-days, and occasionally, Mum goes to the cupboard and there's no porridge there. (Ha, ha!) As soon as Rosie and I have finished dancing around the kitchen, Mum serves us our all-time favourite breakfast. Mum calls it 'bananas and yoghurt', but when Rosie was a baby, she called it 'nana-loggies', and that's what we still call it (when we're not writing cookbooks).

For a real treat, you could mash some fresh strawberries in with the bananas. You could also try sprinkling the finished dish with some flaked almonds.

For each person you will need:
1 banana
1 small pot of yoghurt. (You can try any flavour you like, but our all-time favourite is strawberry.)

What you do:
1. Get out a bowl for each person.
2. Put the banana into the bowl and mash it well. (Don't forget to peel the banana first!)
3. Pour the yoghurt over the mashed banana and stir well. Then eat. Yum!

Tips
The banana needs to be nice and ripe. If it's green, it won't mash very well. If it's too ripe, it will mash beautifully, but who wants to eat brown bananas? Gross!

Tropical Smoothie

Mmm. The flavour, the aroma of this lovely, luscious liquid ...

OK, so you got an A in creative writing — now get on with the recipe. — Megan

For four glasses you will need:
3 passion fruits
1 mango
1 banana
500ml of orange juice (you can squeeze your own or use unsweetened juice from a carton.)

What you do:
1. Take out your electric blender, but don't plug it in until you're ready to blend.
2. Cut the passion fruits in half and use a spoon to scoop the flesh into the jug of the blender.
3. Carefully peel the mango and chop the flesh away from the stone. Add the mango to the blender.
4. Peel the banana, chop it into biggish pieces and add to the blender.
5. Now pour the orange juice into the blender and whizz until everything is well mixed together.
6. Pour into glasses and serve. I like to add one of those cool paper umbrellas to make it REALLY tropical!

These eggs are really nice served with toast.

Baked Eggs

Miss Leonard said we should include a nice easy recipe for fried eggs – 'Anyone can cook fried eggs,' she said. When we tried it out though, I did find someone who couldn't fry an egg. I've been sworn to secrecy, but I'm allowed to say that it went very, very wrong. So instead here's our nice easy recipe for baked eggs. They taste great, and almost anyone could do it.

For each person you will need:

1 egg
1 spring onion
Half a slice of ham
1 dessertspoon of grated cheese
A little oil for greasing

What you do:

1. Get out a ramekin dish (an individual-sized, oven-proof dish) for each person.
2. Preheat your oven to 160 degrees / gas 4.
3. Grease the ramekins.
4. Chop the spring onion and the ham, mix together and put into the bottom of the ramekin.
5. Break the egg on top of the onion and ham. (Try not to break the yolk, but it's not a disaster if that happens — your baked eggs just won't look quite as pretty.)
6. Sprinkle the cheese over the top.
7. Put on a tray in the oven and bake for 10-15 minutes depending on how you like your eggs cooked.

Tips

You can leave out the ham or onions if you like. Leaving out the eggs might be a bit too drastic!

Instead of ham, you could fry some bacon and use that.

Try putting some mushrooms in with the onion and ham.

If you like tomatoes, you could put a few thin slices on top of the grated cheese!

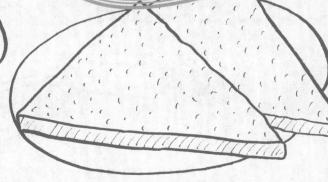

You can eat this as it is, but it's much nicer with toppings. You can try honey, lemon juice or jam. (Louise likes ketchup on hers, but we think that's totally weird.)

For each person you will need:
Two slices of bread
1 (hen's!) egg
1 dessertspoon of milk
A little oil for frying

What you do:
1. Crack the egg into a cup or a small bowl, add the milk and beat well with a fork.
2. Carefully pour the egg and milk mixture onto a dinner plate, and swirl the slices of bread around in it until they are soaked through on both sides.
3. Pour the oil into a large pan and put over a medium heat. After a few minutes, add the eggy bread slices and fry until golden brown. Turn the slices over, and cook the other side until it is brown and the toast is cooked through.
4. Eat!

Hot Cakes

These are a bit like small, fat pancakes.

These are delicious with maple syrup or sprinkled with lemon juice. If you have some blueberries, you could mix them into the batter before cooking, or just serve them on the side.

Fot 10-12 hot cakes you will need:
140g of self-raising flour
A good pinch of bicarbonate of soda (bread soda)
1 level dessertspoon of caster sugar
1 egg
150ml of milk
A little oil for frying

What you do:
1. Get out an electric beater or whisk and a large mixing bowl (if you don't have an electric beater you can use a hand whisk — it will just take a bit longer).
2. Measure the flour, bicarbonate of soda and sugar into the large mixing bowl.
3. Make a well in the flour and sugar mix, and crack the egg into it. ('Make a well' means make a dip or a hole in centre of the flour and sugar mix.)
4. Pour about a third (50ml) of the milk into the well.
5. Using the electric beater at low speed, (or the hand whisk) begin to mix, allowing the flour to gradually fall in from the sides.
6. When the flour is all mixed in, gradually add the rest of the milk. Turn up the speed of the mixer and beat for a few minutes (or just beat faster with the hand whisk — the exercise is good for you).
7. Put the mixture into the fridge for half an hour, while you clean the spatters from the ceiling. (Just kidding about the spatters! Go and check your text messages or something.)
8. After half an hour, heat the oil in a large frying pan, over a medium-high heat. Once the oil is hot, use a ladle to spoon dollops of the mixture onto the pan, allowing them to spread out. You should have room for three or four at a time. As soon as the surface of each cake begins to bubble, turn the cakes with a spatula, and cook the other side for a minute or two. Remove from pan, and keep them warm while you cook the rest.

Tips
As a special treat for Rosie, I sometimes make 'face-cakes'. All I do is this: Remove a dessertspoon of the batter, and mix it up with some cocoa powder. When the first side of the pancake is cooking, use a spoon to make a face shape by dropping blobs of the cocoa-flavoured mixture onto the uncooked side. Turn over and cook as usual. The face usually looks like a person who's gone a few rounds with a very tough boxer, but Rosie never minds!

Special Sausage Rolls

These are made with sliced bread instead of pastry, and they are totally delicious.

These are yummy with tomato sauce or mustard.

For eight sausage rolls you will need:
40g of butter
4 slices of very fresh white bread
30g of cheddar cheese
4 sausages

What you do:

1. Switch on the oven to 180 degrees / gas 6. Put the butter into a small bowl, then put it into the oven to melt. (Be careful taking the bowl out of the oven as it will be hot!)

2. While the butter is melting, cut the crusts from the bread. Don't waste the crusts!

Save them for making stuffing, or if that's too hard, throw them into the garden to feed the birds. — Sheila

3. Grate the cheese.

4. By now the butter should be melted. Take the bowl out of the oven. Put the bread on a board, and use a pastry brush or the back of a spoon to brush the butter all over both sides of the bread.

5. Put one sausage along the short edge of each slice of bread. Sprinkle the cheese over the sausages.

6. Roll up the bread tightly so that the cheese and sausages are covered. This is a messy job. Don't be afraid to squish the bread tightly with your fingers — if you don't, the rolls won't stay together.

7. Cut each roll in half so you end up with eight small sausage rolls.

8. Put the rolls onto a baking try, with the overlapping edges of bread facing down.

9. Put the tray of sausage rolls into the oven and cook for thirty minutes until the bread is golden and the sausages are cooked through. (You can test one by cutting it in half.)

10. Eat!

Yummy Yoghurt Parfait

I love the fancy yoghurts that come in two matching pots that you have to stir together. Mum never buys them though, as she says they're too expensive, and just a gimmick. ('Gimmick' is one of her favourite words.) Then Mum invented this breakfast, and everyone was happy.

For each person you will need:

Some soft fruit — raspberries, strawberries, blueberries, for example.

1 small tub of your favourite yoghurt

1 teaspoon of honey

1 dessertspoonful of porridge oats

What you do:

1. Put the fruit into a dessert bowl (or a glass, if you're feeling very fancy).

2. Spoon the yoghurt over the fruit.

3. Sprinkle the oats over the yoghurt.

4. Drizzle the honey over the top and eat!

Tips

If you like nuts, you could chop some and add with the oats.

If you want, you could cook the fruit with a little water before making this breakfast — this warmer breakfast of stewed fruit and yoghurt is great on cold winter mornings.

This works well as a dessert too — or you could pack it in a plastic tub and bring it to school for lunch.

Sheila's Porridge

Megan's always going on and on about hating porridge, so when we were going to France, I did her a favour and hid the porridge in her garage before we left. In the end, though, I was kind of sorry, because I think porridge is yummy. (And if Sheila reads this, I'm going to be really, really sorry about hiding the porridge, as she never found out the truth!)

You only say that because you haven't had it every morning for ten years — that's 3,650 bowls of porridge so far — not funny — Megan

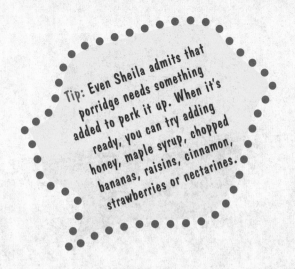

Tip: Even Sheila admits that porridge needs something added to perk it up. When it's ready, you can try adding honey, maple syrup, chopped bananas, raisins, cinnamon, strawberries or nectarines.

For each lucky person you will need:

350ml of liquid (this can be milk or water or a mixture of the two) (This does not work with orange juice or coke — I know, because I've tried them.)

90g of porridge oats

A topping of your choice (see 'Tip')

What you do:

1. Pour the liquid into a saucepan, add the oats, and stir over a medium heat until it is simmering. Allow to simmer for about 5-7 minutes, stirring occasionally, and adding a little more liquid if it looks like it's getting too thick.

2. That's it! Pour it into a bowl and eat it.

Strawberry & Banana Smoothie

Yummy and good for you. What more could you ask for?

For four smoothies you will need:

1 banana
200g of fresh strawberries
250g of vanilla yoghurt
200ml of milk

What you do:
1. Take out your electric blender, but don't plug it in until you're ready to blend.
2. Wash the strawberries, and cut off the green tops. Peel the banana.
3. Now put all the fruit, the yoghurt and the milk into the blender, put on the lid and whizz until smooth. (Remember to turn off the blender and unplug it once you've finished blending — no one wants fingers blended into their smoothie!)
4. Drink immediately. Delicious!

Granola

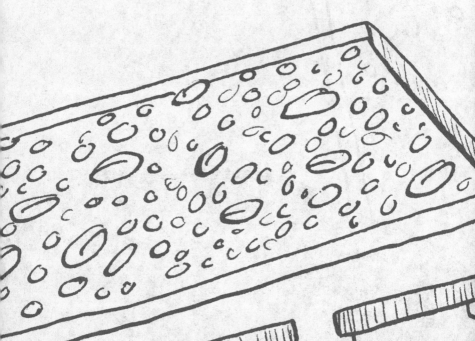

NUTS

SEEDS

To make enough for lots of yummy breakfasts, you will need:

300g of porridge oats
50g of sunflower seeds
1 tablespoon of pumpkin seeds
100g mixed nuts (not salted)
60ml of sunflower oil
2 tablespoons of honey

Serve this in cereal bowls with ice-cold milk.

What you do:
1. Preheat the oven to 140 degrees / gas 3.
2. Fill a saucepan with boiling water, place it over a medium heat on the cooker and allow it to simmer.
3. Measure the honey and the oil into a cup. Stand the cup in the saucepan of simmering water, stirring occasionally, until the honey has softened.
4. Mix all the dry ingredients — the oats, seeds and nuts — in a large bowl. Add the warm oil and honey mix, and stir well.
5. Spread the mixture out on a large baking tray, place in the oven and cook for 50 — 60 minutes. After 25 minutes, take the tray from the oven, stir the contents and then return the tray to the oven.
6. When the granola is lightly browned, take the tray out of the oven, and allow the mixture to cool, stirring occasionally. When it is fully cool, store in an airtight container until breakfast time

Tip
If you like dried fruit like raisins and apricots, you can add these when serving. Don't store soft fruit with the granola though, as the fruit will make it go soft.

I used to complain a lot about the lunches my mum made for me, but then I met Marcus, who had no-one to make lunches for him, and I realised how lucky I was. Sometimes, though, the suspense is too much for me. You can imagine what it's like. It's break time, you feel like you haven't eaten in days, and you have no idea what's in your lunch-box. You peel open the lid, hardly daring to hope that it's going to be something nice ...

Why not take control and prepare your own lunch sometimes? It's fun, and you'll know for sure that you're going to like it.

Pasta Salad

This quantity makes enough for one generous portion. You can easily double or triple it. Just keep it in an airtight container in the fridge for a day or two until you are ready to use it.

SWE

I brought this for lunch last week and all my friends were jealous.

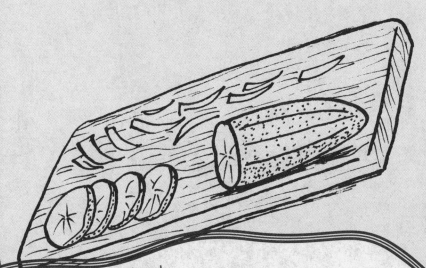

For each person you will need:
50g of your favourite dry pasta shapes
2 tablespoons of sweetcorn, from a can or frozen (it defrosts quickly)
1 tablespoon of finely chopped red onion
1 dessertspoon of mayonnaise
1 teaspoon of pesto

What you do:
1. Cook the pasta according to the instructions on the packet. Drain, and set aside to cool.
2. Put the sweetcorn, the chopped onion and the cooled pasta into a bowl and mix.
3. Mix the pesto and mayonnaise together in a cup. Add to the other ingredients, and stir well.

Tips
You can have fun with this recipe, adding lots of your favourite salad ingredients. Try any or all of these — chopped cherry tomatoes, chopped cucumber, chopped spring onions, pine-nuts ... the list is endless!
If you want to make it more substantial, you could add some tinned tuna, cooked salmon or shredded cooked chicken.

Fruit Boxes

An apple or a banana is a nice easy
And healthy! – Sheila snack for school,
but sometimes you feel like something
a bit more exciting. The only problem
about these boxes of fruit is keeping
your friends away (you know who I
mean, Louise), so always bring a bit
more than you think you will need.

What you will need:
Fresh pineapple
Fresh melon
Grapes
Mandarin oranges

What you do:
1. Carefully cut two slices from the pineapple. Cut off the skin, and cut out the core. Chop the remainder into big chunks.
2. Cut the melon in half and scrape out the seeds. Slice the melon and then remove the skin by running a knife carefully along the bottom of the slices, just under the skin.
3. Chop the melon slices into chunks.
4. Wash the grapes.
5. Peel and divide the mandarin into segments.
6. Pile all the fruit into a lunch box with a tight-fitting lid, and do your best not to touch it until break-time!

Tips
1. You can try lots of different fruit for this — strawberries, mango, watermelon, etc. Don't use apples or bananas — they might go brown and that's too gross for words.
2. If you're not a morning person, you can prepare this the night before, and keep it in the fridge until you're ready to go to school.

43

Sandwiches

The sandwich was named after the fourth Earl of Sandwich, who asked his servants to bring him meat wrapped in bread, so he wouldn't get his hands dirty while he played cards. (Or so the Internet says.)

OK, so sandwiches aren't the most exciting things in the world, but they're quick to make, they fill you up, and they're good for you, so who are we to complain? You can liven them up by varying the bread you use – white, brown, French, *Dreaming of Bruno! – Megan* pitta and ciabatta are all good.

But, like with people, it's what's inside that counts, so be creative with your fillings. We asked lots of people to share their favourite sandwich fillings with us, and this is what we got. Try them, and see who you agree with.

Louise: grated carrot, grated cheese and grated apple, all mixed together with a drop of French dressing or mayonnaise.

Grace: sliced chicken, brie and cranberry sauce. (Very fancy.)

Kellie: tuna, cucumber, spring onion and mayonnaise.

Megan's mum: hummus and roasted peppers.

Megan's dad: spicy chicken.

Rosie: just cheese!

Aunt Linda: goat's cheese and sundried tomatoes.

Alice's mum: ham, cheese and sweet chilli sauce.

Alice's dad; sliced hard-boiled eggs with tomatoes, mayo and cress.

Jamie: cheese and onion crisps. (Well, you didn't expect him to pick something healthy did you?)

Miss Leonard: cream cheese, smoked salmon and iceberg lettuce. (She's just showing off!)

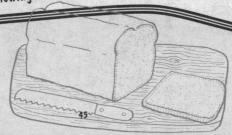

Yummy Dip

Simple, but delicious — only let your friends taste it if you are very, very good at sharing.

What you will need:
1 tablespoon of Philadelphia (or your favourite brand of) soft cheese
1 dessertspoon of sweet chilli sauce
Vegetable sticks for dipping: carrots, peppers, celery, cucumber

What you do:
1. Put the cheese into a small plastic container with a lid.
2. Pour over some sweet chilli sauce so it covers the top of the cheese and drips down the sides. Stir a little bit. Put on the lid.
3. Prepare your vegetables, and pack them in a separate container.
4. When lunchtime comes, start dipping.

Breadsticks are really nice with this dip, but pack them separately or they will be soft by lunch-time — totally gross!

Wraps

Sandwiches are great, but sometimes you get tired of them, and then it's time to reach for the wraps. They're delicious, and once you get the hang of rolling them, you could do it in your sleep.

How to roll a wrap:

1. Fill flat wrap

2. Fold in top ends

3. Roll into nice parcel shape

4. Turn over; flat side down

What you do:

1. Lay your wrap on a flat surface, and pile the filling right in the middle in the shape of a fat sausage (horizontally).
2. Turn the ends of the wrap in.
3. Now roll up from one side so you have a neat parcel shape.
4. If you are serving your wrap immediately, it looks nice if you use a sharp knife to cut it in half diagonally.
5. If it's for your lunchbox, it holds together better if you leave it whole, and wrap tightly in cling-film.

Fillings:

Turkey (or chicken) and mayo:

Chop some cooked turkey or chicken into small cubes. Add some finely chopped red onion and sweetcorn. Stir in some mayonnaise and it's ready. I love pesto, so I stir in a little of that with the mayo. It's delicious — Grace

Tuna and carrot:

Mix up a can of tuna with grated carrot, finely chopped celery, spring onions and mayo.

Hummus and roasted red pepper:

Mix up hummus, sliced strips of roasted red pepper (from a jar) and some toasted pine nuts.

Ham and cheese:

Mix together some grated cheddar cheese, finely chopped spring onions, chopped ham and mayonnaise.

You can add shredded lettuce to any of the fillings suggested.

We're suggesting four fillings, but there are heaps more. Use your imagination and put in the stuff you like — after all, it's your lunch! The trick is to make sure that your filling is not too dry, nor too runny. You can make enough filling for a few days, and keep it in the fridge, but it's best to assemble your wrap on the day you want to eat it — soggy wraps so aren't cool!

Raspberry Muffins

When I open my lunch-box and find one of these, the whole day starts to get better.

For twelve small muffins you will need:

110g of plain flour
One and a half teaspoons of baking powder
A large pinch of bread soda
One quarter teaspoon of ground cinnamon
A large pinch of salt
50g of wholemeal flour
50g of brown sugar

1 egg
50ml of natural yoghurt
50ml of milk
40ml of sunflower oil
Half a teaspoon of vanilla extract
125g of fresh raspberries (or frozen raspberries, defrosted)

What you do:
1. Line a regular sized bun tin with 12 bun cases.
2. Preheat the oven to 180 degrees / gas 6.
3. Sieve the plain flour, cinnamon, baking powder, bread soda and salt into a large bowl. Add the wholemeal flour and the sugar and stir everything together.
4. Break the egg into another large bowl and whisk with a hand whisk. Add the yoghurt, milk, sunflower oil and vanilla extract and whisk until everything is well mixed.
5. Wash the raspberries and cut them in half. Stir them into the egg/milk mixture.
6. Now pour the dry mixture into the wet mixture and mix gently until just barely blended. (If you over-mix muffins, they go tough and heavy. We found that out the hard way, but all you have to do is listen to us!)
7. Spoon the mixture into the bun cases, and bake for 12-14 minutes. Allow to cool on a wire rack.

Tips
If you like, you can use large muffin cases for these. They will take a while longer to cook, and of course you won't get twelve of them. Raspberries are our absolute favourite fruit for these, but if you're feeling experimental, you could try them with blueberries or blackberries or even some grated eating apples.

Muesli Bars

Sugary liquids can burn you, so be very careful not to get splashed.

For sixteen muesli bars you will need:
100g of light brown sugar
100g of butter
3 tablespoons of golden syrup
350g of sugar-free muesli
100g of mixed unsalted nuts
A square baking tin with sides of about 23cm. Rectangular tins work too, just do the maths to see if yours is the right size. (Circular tins make cutting the bars a bit difficult.)
A little oil or butter for greasing and parchment for lining your tin

What you do:
1. Preheat your oven to 160 degrees / gas 4.
2. Prepare your tin by greasing it with butter or oil, and then line it with baking parchment. (Don't skip this step unless you want to end up eating your muesli bars with a spoon straight from the tin.)
3. Put the sugar, butter and syrup into a large saucepan, and heat until the butter is melted and the sugar has dissolved. Be careful not to burn yourself.
4. Carefully chop the nuts into large chunks.
5. Pour the nuts and muesli into the sugar/butter mix, and stir until everything is well combined.
6. Tip the mixture into the prepared cake tin, and press down well with the back of a spoon (or a potato masher.)
7. Bake for about 20 minutes until it is turning brown at the edges.
8. Leave to cool in the tin. When fully cool, carefully remove from the tin using the baking parchment. Peel off the parchment and carefully cut your mix into slices to make muesli bars.
9. Store the bars in an airtight container until ready to eat.

Broccoli & Carrot Salad

For two portions you will need:
6 large florets of broccoli
1 large carrot
1 dessertspoon of mayonnaise
Two pinches of curry powder
1 small packet of salted peanuts

What you do:
1. Wash the broccoli, chop it into small pieces and put it into a bowl.
2. Scrape the carrot, and cut it into small dice. Add to the broccoli.
3. Put the mayonnaise into a cup, and stir in the curry powder. When it's well mixed, add to the veg and stir well.
4. Add the peanuts and stir again.
5. Pack into airtight plastic containers and store in the fridge.

Tip
This is nice for lunchboxes, but it's also good as a side dish with any of our main courses.

Fat Biscuits served with Cheddar

Even though these biscuits are slightly sweet, they are totally delicious when eaten with slices of cheddar cheese. Sounds weird, but you'll have to trust us.

What you will need for 10-12 lovely biscuits:
75g of plain flour
75g of wholemeal flour
50g of caster sugar
100g of butter, cut into chunks
A little oil or butter for greasing
Some slices of cheddar cheese, to serve

What you do:
1. Preheat the oven to 180 degrees / gas 6. Grease a large flat baking tray.
2. Put the first four ingredients into a large mixing bowl.
3. Use your fingers to rub the butter into the other ingredients. See 'Tips & Techniques' p15. Keep rubbing until it looks like very small breadcrumbs. Now use your fingers to squish it all together. I'm good at this – it's like playing with Play-doh at playschool – Rosie (Unless you have giant-sized hands, then it's probably easiest to squish into two separate lumps.)
4. Dust your work surface with flour, and put one lump of mixture on top. Use your fingers to flatten it to about the thickness of your little finger.
5. Use your favourite shaped cutter to cut the dough into shapes, and put these onto your prepared baking tray.
6. Repeat with the other lump, and then roll the scraps together and cut those out too.
7. Cook for 10-15 minutes until golden brown. Use a spatula to lift the cookies from the tray onto a wire rack to cool.
8. For school, pack a biscuit or two in one container, and some sliced cheese in another, and put together when you are ready to eat.

Tip
If you like, you can top the cheese and biscuits with some sliced grapes.
Rosie likes these biscuits spread with strawberry jam.

Swirly Scones

As this is for school lunches and you might want to make them quickly, we've cheated and used scone mix from a packet. If you've got lots of time, you could look up a recipe for home-made scones and use that mixture instead.

What you will need:

1 pack of white scone mix
150g of tomato sauce (use some from the recipe on page 98 or cheat again and use some pasta sauce from a jar)
3 tablespoons of grated cheese
4 finely chopped spring onions
A little flour for rolling out the dough
A little oil or butter for greasing

What you do:

1. Preheat the oven to the temperature indicated on the scone packet.
2. Grease two flat baking sheets with a little oil or butter.
3. Prepare the scone dough according to the packet instructions.
4. Sprinkle your work surface with flour, and roll out the dough into a rectangle about 1cm thick.
5. Spread the tomato sauce onto the dough. Then sprinkle the cheese and chopped onions on top of the sauce.
6. Carefully roll the dough up like a Swiss roll, then cut it into slices about 1 1/2cm thick.
7. Lay the slices onto the greased baking sheets and cook according to the instructions on the scone packet.
8. When cooked, use a fish slice to lift the swirls onto a wire rack to cool.

Children need regular feeding, so if your next mealtime isn't for hours, resist the urge to eat your homework, and try one of these snacks. Suitable for sleepovers, after-school, wet Wednesdays or just whenever. Have fun!

Super Snacks

Chicken & Sweetcorn Soup

Always use a separate chopping board & knife for raw meat!

Always make sure chicken is well cooked; there must be no pink at all left!

For four people you will need:
1 large boneless, skinless chicken breast
4 spring onions
3cm piece of fresh ginger
2 cloves of garlic
340g can of sweetcorn
500ml of chicken stock (fresh or made from a stock cube)
A dash of soy sauce
Black pepper
A little oil for frying

What you do:
1. Wash and finely chop the spring onions.
2. Peel and finely chop the ginger.
3. Peel and finely chop (or crush) the garlic.
4. Pour a little oil into a large saucepan and heat it. Add the chopped vegetables and cook for about 2 minutes until soft, but not brown.
5. Drain the sweetcorn, and add to the saucepan with the chicken stock. Bring to a simmer.
6. While the soup is simmering, chop the chicken breast as finely as you can. (You should be aiming for something that looks like minced chicken.)
7. Add the chicken to the soup and simmer for five minutes until the chicken is cooked. This doesn't take long, as the chicken is (or should be!) so fine.
8. Add a dash of soy sauce, a grind of black pepper, and serve.

Warm Salad

When I see this salad, it reminds me a bit of the salad we made for my dad and your Aunt Linda — Alice

Trust me, this salad is nothing like that. This salad is nice!

— Megan

Always make sure chicken is well cooked; there must be no pink at all left!

Always use a
separate chopping
board & knife for
raw meat!

For four people you will need:
2 boneless skinless chicken breasts
A little oil for frying
1 small head of lettuce or a small bag of mixed salad leaves
About a quarter of a cucumber
12 cherry tomatoes
Sweet chilli sauce

What you do:

1. Heat a little oil in a frying pan. Chop the chicken into small chunks, add to the pan when the oil is hot and fry until cooked all the way through. Keep warm.
2. Wash and dry the lettuce and arrange on four plates.
3. Get out a clean chopping board for the vegetables. Wash and slice the cucumber, and arrange on top of the lettuce.
4. Wash the tomatoes, cut in half, and add to the salad plates.
5. Add the warm chicken to the salad.
6. Drizzle the whole lot with a little sweet chilli sauce, and eat while the chicken is still warm.

Tips

You can add all kinds of stuff to this salad — try chopped spring onions, sunflower seeds, chopped celery, etc.

Slightly Spicy Lentil Soup
by Sheila

Lentils are healthy and delicious, and I offered to write a whole section on lentil recipes, but for some reason, Megan wasn't keen ...

Er ... that's because we actually hope to sell some of these books – Megan

Ignore Megan, this soup is totally delicious. And beside, lentils always make me happy – they remind me of the lentil stew I poured over that evil Pascal's head in France – Alice

For 4-6 people you will need:
1 tablespoon of olive oil
1 onion
2 cloves of garlic
Half a teaspoon of ground coriander
Half a teaspoon of ground cumin
120g of dried split red lentils
1 litre chicken stock
A squeeze of lemon juice
Salt & pepper

What you do:
1. Heat the oil in a large saucepan. Chop the onion as finely as you can, add to the pan, and cook on a low heat until the onion is soft, but not brown.
2. Peel and finely chop (or crush) the garlic. Add to the pan with the cumin and coriander. Stir and heat for 1 minute.
3. Add the chicken stock and the lentils and stir well. Bring to the boil, then turn down the heat, cover and simmer for 35-45 minutes.
4. Squeeze in a little lemon juice, and add some salt and pepper if you think it needs it.
5. Serve with some home-made brown bread (see p 150), or your favourite white bread.

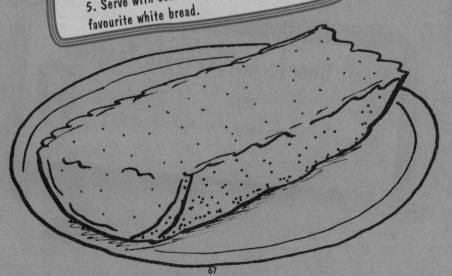

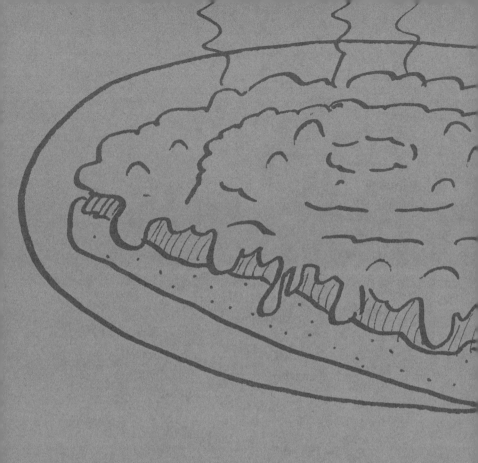

Ham, Cheese & Pineapple Toasties

This is a really easy recipe, as all the ingredients are in the title!

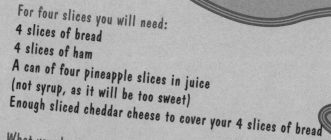

For four slices you will need:
4 slices of bread
4 slices of ham
A can of four pineapple slices in juice
(not syrup, as it will be too sweet)
Enough sliced cheddar cheese to cover your 4 slices of bread

What you do:
1. Turn on your grill and toast one side of the slices of bread until golden brown.
2. Turn over the bread, and put the slices of ham onto the untoasted sides.
3. Drain the pineapple slices (drink the juice if you like, but not from the can — that hurts!)
4. Put one slice of pineapple on top of each slice of ham.
5. Top with the cheese slices.
6. Put back under the grill until bubbling nicely and just starting to brown.
7. Eat.

Potato & Bacon Soup

This is really quick and really, really delicious.

Always use a separate chopping board & knife for raw meat!

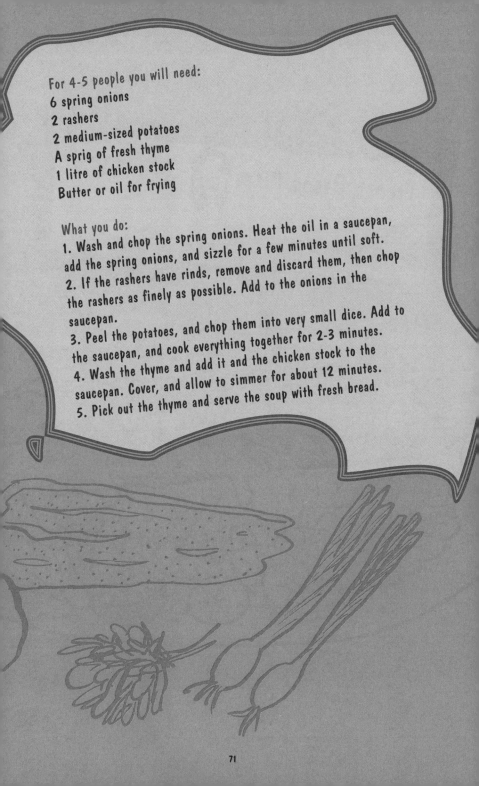

For 4-5 people you will need:
6 spring onions
2 rashers
2 medium-sized potatoes
A sprig of fresh thyme
1 litre of chicken stock
Butter or oil for frying

What you do:
1. Wash and chop the spring onions. Heat the oil in a saucepan, add the spring onions, and sizzle for a few minutes until soft.
2. If the rashers have rinds, remove and discard them, then chop the rashers as finely as possible. Add to the onions in the saucepan.
3. Peel the potatoes, and chop them into very small dice. Add to the saucepan, and cook everything together for 2-3 minutes.
4. Wash the thyme and add it and the chicken stock to the saucepan. Cover, and allow to simmer for about 12 minutes.
5. Pick out the thyme and serve the soup with fresh bread.

French Bread Pizza

Totally yummy!

For four people you will need:
A piece of French bread (about 50cm long)
1 medium-sized onion
2 regular tomatoes (or a handful of cherry tomatoes)
Half a red pepper (optional)
120g of grated cheddar cheese
A little oil for frying

What you do:
1. Finely chop the onion, tomatoes and red pepper (if using).
2. Heat the oil in a saucepan, and add the chopped vegetables.
3. Cook the vegetables over a medium heat, until slightly softened, but not brown.
4. Add the grated cheese to the saucepan with the vegetables, and stir until melted. Switch off the heat and set aside.
5. Turn on the grill to high. Cut the French bread into four equal chunks and then cut each chunk in half lengthways. (If you're good at maths, this will give you eight chunks of bread — two for each person.)
6. Grill the bread, turning once, so both sides are golden brown and toasty. (Don't send texts while the bread is grilling; it always burns while you're not looking.)
7. Put the bread onto a board, cut side up. Use a spoon to spread the cheesy mix over the browned surface. Return to the grill for a minute, until the cheese is just starting to bubble.
8. Sit back, think of Bruno, and enjoy!

Tip
If you like, you can top with your favourite herbs before the final grilling.

Quesadillas are nice on their own, or served with ketchup or sweet chilli sauce.

Quesadillas

These are quick to make and very tasty. I often make these on Friday nights, when I want to use up any tortilla wraps leftover from making my school lunches. Each quesadilla will serve two people (or one very hungry person).

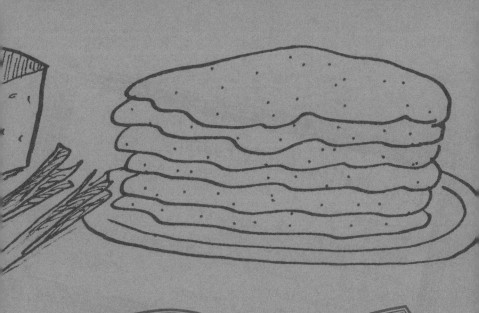

For each quesadilla you will need:
2 tortilla wraps
About 100g of grated cheese
2 chopped spring onions

What you do:
1. Put a large non-stick frying pan on a medium heat, without any oil.
2. Put one tortilla on the pan, and sprinkle the grated cheese and chopped onions over it.
3. Place the other tortilla on top, and press down carefully with a spatula, or potato masher.
4. As soon as the cheese starts to melt, use a spatula to carefully turn the quesadilla over, and cook the other side until it is lightly brown, and the cheese is fully melted.
5. Lift the quesadilla onto a board, cut into wedges and serve.

Alternative (and totally delicious) filling:
Spread the upper side of your first tortilla with cranberry sauce. Add some shredded cooked chicken, and a few slices of brie. Cook as above and serve.

Choc-Mallow Petits Fours

In case you didn't know, 'petits fours' are small, sweet treats served at the end of a meal.

The name is French and it means 'little oven'. I learned that when I was in France.

That's not all you learned — remember Bruno?? — Alice

Small and sweet, just like me! — Rosie

For ten *Petits Fours* you will need:

A 100g bar of milk chocolate

10 regular-sized marshmallows or 20 mini-marshmallows

10 *petits fours* cases (not that fancy — they're just baby-sized bun cases.)

What you do:

1. Break up the chocolate and put into a small bowl over a pan of simmering water. Stir until the chocolate is melted. ('Tips & Techniques', p 15.)

2. Put the *petits fours* cases onto a flat tray or a big plate. Put a teaspoonful of melted chocolate into each paper case.

3. Place one regular or two mini marshmallows into the soft chocolate in each paper case, pressing down gently.

4. Use the scrapings of the chocolate bowl (if you haven't licked it clean by now) to put one dot of chocolate on top of each marshmallow.

5. Put into the fridge to set, and find something very exciting to do to distract you while you are waiting! They should be ready in an hour or two and then you can invite your nine very best friends over to visit.

Real Hot Chocolate

Hot chocolate has to be the nicest drink in the whole wide world. Once Linda took the two of us and Rosie out for hot chocolate, and it was so delicious that Rosie asked for a cup of it from Santa that year.

For each person you will need:
150 ml of milk
25g of chocolate (can be white, or dark, but our favourite is milk chocolate.)
A few marshmallows

What you do:
1. Grate the chocolate or chop it as small as you can.
2. Put the chocolate and the milk into a saucepan, and stir over a medium heat until the chocolate has dissolved.
3. Pour the hot chocolate into pretty mugs, and float the marshmallows on top.

Tip
To make it look and taste even better, you can dust the finished drink with a little cocoa or drinking chocolate powder.

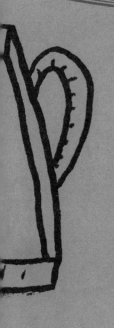

S'Mores

So-called because when you eat them, there's only one thing to say – 'some more / s'more' – geddit? Miss Leonard says this doesn't count as a proper recipe, but she's only saying that because she's never tasted how totally, totally delicious they are.

When I was in summer camp, I met a really nice girl called Sarah, and she told me how to make these.

For each s'more you will need:

2 digestive biscuits
2 squares of milk chocolate
1 marshmallow

What you do:

1. Turn on the grill to medium.
2. Put the marshmallow on one biscuit, and the chocolate squares on the other.
3. Put the biscuits on a rack and grill until the chocolate is softening, and the marshmallow is just starting to turn brown — that means that the inside will be totally delicious and squidgy inside. You need to watch them carefully, as chocolate and marshmallows burn easily — just ask **Alice.**

You promised you wouldn't put that bit in. Mum forgave me in the end — Alice

4. Remove from the grill, and carefully squish the biscuits together.
5. Eat carefully, as the inside can be quite hot.
6. Lick your lips and say, 'S'more, please.'

Marvellous Main Courses

Chicken & Pasta

Always use a separate chopping board & knife for raw meat!

Always make sure chicken is well cooked; there must be no pink at all left!

This is really delicious with some parmesan, or your favourite hard cheese, grated over it.

For four people you will need:
Four chicken breasts, chopped into small, even-sized chunks
A bunch of spring onions
2 rashers
Four handfuls of frozen peas or sweetcorn (or a mixture of both)
Four portions of your favourite pasta
2 heaped tablespoons of crème fraiche
Oil for frying
Freshly-ground black pepper (optional)
Some freshly-chopped parsley (optional)

What you do:
1. Heat some oil in a wok or large frying pan over a medium heat. Add the chopped chicken and fry for 10 minutes until fully cooked. Scoop the chicken out of the wok, set aside and keep warm.
2. Chop the rashers and the spring onions into small pieces. Put into the wok or pan, with a little more oil if necessary. Add the sweetcorn and/or peas. Cook for 5-6 minutes.
3. While the rashers, onions and sweetcorn / peas are cooking, put your pasta on to cook according to the packet instructions.
4. Return the chicken to the wok, with the crème fraiche, and stir everything around over the heat for a minute or two.
5. Drain the pasta, and add to the wok. Add the black pepper and the parsley (if using). Stir everything together.
6. Serve.

Tips
If you like your food really gloopy, you can save a few tablespoons of the pasta water, and add it with the crème fraiche.

Home-Made Beef Burgers

I like these because they taste much, much better than take-away ones – Megan

I like these because they are much, much healthier than take-away ones – Sheila

Always make sure mince is well cooked; there must be no pink at all left!

For four burgers you will need:
300g of minced beef
1 onion
Fresh thyme and parsley (if you have them)
A little oil for frying
Some trimmings — burger buns, lettuce, grated cheese, sliced onions, sliced tomatoes, ketchup, mayonnaise — you can add gherkins, mustard, whatever you like!

What you do:
1. Put the minced beef into a big bowl.
2. Wash your hands after touching the raw meat, and then chop the first onion as finely as you can (if it's in big chunks, the burgers won't stick together very well). Add the onion to the meat.
3. If you're using herbs, chop them finely and add them with some freshly-ground black pepper.
4. Now use your hands to mix everything together very well.
5. Divide the mixture into four and shape into burgers. The easiest way is to squish the mixture into four balls first, then put them on a board and flatten them into burger shapes.
6. Heat a little oil in a frying pan, and add the burgers. Again, wash your hands after handling the raw meat. Fry the burgers for 6-8 minutes on one side, then use a spatula to carefully turn them over, and cook the second side for another 6-8 minutes. Resist the urge to push them around the pan or they will break up. Cut one burger, to make sure that it isn't pink inside. If it is pink, cook for another few minutes.
7. Put the burgers into the oven to keep them warm while you grill the cut sides of the burger buns.
8. Get your trimmings together, and let everyone assemble their burgers, using the stuff they like.
9. Eat!

Sizzling Stir Fry

This is really nice served with noodles or rice. Just read the instructions on the packet, and put them on to cook so that they will be ready at the same time as the stir-fry. If you like, you can cook some chicken strips, beef strips or prawns, and add to the vegetables with the stock and stir until everything is mixed up.

For four people you will need:
5 spring onions (or one small onion)
4 cloves of garlic (to make it taste nice, and to keep vampires away)

Who wants to keep vampires away – haven't you seen Twilight? – Alice

1 red chilli
3cm piece of fresh root ginger
One red pepper
2 small carrots
A big handful of mangetout (or French beans or runner beans or a few broccoli florets)
One dessertspoon of soy sauce
One dessertspoon of sesame oil (optional)
350ml of chicken stock or vegetable stock
A little oil for frying

What you do:
1. Prepare the vegetables. Peel and chop the onions. Peel and chop the garlic. Peel and chop the ginger. Wash and chop the chillies, discarding the seeds unless you like very hot food. (Be careful not to touch your eyes after chopping chillies – not funny.) Scrape the carrots and chop them into sticks. Wash and prepare whatever green vegetables you are using.
2. Heat some oil in a wok or big frying pan and add the vegetables. Stir-fry for few minutes until warm, but still crunchy on the inside.
3. Add the stock, the soy sauce and the sesame oil (if using). Stir everything together until it's well mixed and bubbling.
4. Serve with your prepared rice or noodles.

Tip
You can use lots of different vegetables for this. Try mushrooms, shredded red or white cabbage, bean-sprouts, leeks ...

We'd go on, but we have a deadline to meet – Megan

You could also add some cashew nuts or pine nuts.

Meatballs in Tomato Sauce

These meatballs are really nice with the tomato sauce on page 98. If you're in a hurry though, you could use a large jar of tomato sauce (not ketchup!) from the supermarket.

Always make sure mince is well cooked; there must be no pink at all left!

Serve with your favourite pasta, and maybe some nice, crusty bread.

Always wash your hands carefully after handling raw meat.

For 4-6 people you will need:
1 batch of tomato sauce (see page 98) (or a large jar of tomato sauce)
400g of minced beef
2 tablespoons of milk
2 slices of bread (without crusts)
1 onion
4 cloves of garlic
Some chopped thyme and parsley (Fresh is nice, but dried will
do if that's all you have.)
1 egg
3cm piece of fresh ginger, peeled and grated (or chopped finely)
A little black pepper
2 dessertspoons of plain flour
A little oil for frying

What you do:
1. Make the tomato sauce (or else open the jar of sauce and pour into a large
saucepan). While the sauce is cooking, you can prepare the meatballs.
2. Put the milk into a large bowl, and crumble the bread into it. Leave to soak
for a few minutes.
3. Peel and finely chop the onions and garlic, then heat a little oil in a frying pan.
4. Add the onions and garlic to the pan and cook for 5 minutes until soft, but
not brown. Take the pan off the heat when they are soft.
5. Squish up the milky bread with your (clean) fingers, and then add the cooked
onions and garlic to the bowl.
6. Now add the minced beef, the chopped herbs, the ginger and a grind of pepper.
7. Crack the egg into a cup, and beat with a fork, and add that too.
8. Now for the fun part: use your fingers to mix everything up well. Then shape
the mixture into balls about the size of a quail's egg (or a very, very small hen's egg).
9. Put the flour onto a large plate. Roll each meatball in the flour.
10. When the sauce is nearly ready, add a little more oil to the frying pan you
used for the garlic and onions, add the meatballs and fry until browned all over.
Now add the browned meatballs to the tomato sauce, bring to a simmer, cover and
cook for 25 minutes until the meatballs are cooked through. Add a little water
if it looks too dry.
11. Serve with pasta or bread. Enjoy!

Melissa's (Surprisingly Delicious) Chicken by Melissa

Last week we met Melissa and made the big mistake of telling her about our recipe book. She went on and on about this really cool chicken dish that the chef in her fancy boarding school makes. We pretended to be interested, and she gave us the recipe. It was so delicious, we've already made it three times. — Megan

This is nice served with green salad, coleslaw, rice, pasta or potato wedges.

Always use a separate chopping board & knife for raw meat!

For four people you will need:
4 boneless, skinless chicken breasts
1 egg
2 cloves of garlic
Black pepper
100g of fresh breadcrumbs
2 tablespoons of grated parmesan cheese
2 tablespoons of finely chopped parsley
Oil or butter for greasing

Always make sure chicken is well cooked; there must be no pink at all left!

What you do:
1. Grease a large flat baking tray with oil or butter.
2. Cut each chicken breast into about four long, fat strips.
3. Beat the egg, and pour it into a large shallow dish.
4. Peel and crush the garlic and add to the egg.
5. Grind black pepper into the egg and garlic mixture.
6. Add the chicken strips to the egg mixture. Cover and leave in the fridge for half an hour.
7. After half an hour, heat the oven to 190 degrees / gas 7.
8. Mix together the breadcrumbs, parmesan and parsley in a large bowl. When well-mixed, pour on to a large plate.
9. Roll the pieces of eggy chicken in the breadcrumb mix until it's well-coated.
10. Put the coated chicken on the trays, and cook for 20 minutes, turning once.
11. Check that the chicken is cooked through, by cutting the biggest piece in half and making sure that there's no trace of pink left. If it's not quite cooked, return to the oven for another few minutes.
12. Serve.

Tips
If you have any chicken left over (never happens in our house!) it's really nice in sandwiches, with some salad or chopped red onion and mayonnaise.

Flaky Fish Fingers

Miss Leonard said that we should try out these recipes on ~~guinea pigs~~ friends. So Megan and I made these fish fingers for Grace, Louise and Kellie. Louise says she hates fish, but she scoffed hers in seconds, and even took another piece when she thought we weren't looking.

Serve with salad and something nice to dip the fish fingers in. Sweet chilli sauce, mayo and ketchup are all nice.

For four people you will need:
5-6 large handfuls of cornflakes
8 skinless fish-finger sized pieces of firm white fish like cod or haddock. (Ask at the fish counter and they will prepare it for you.)
1 egg
1 tablespoon of milk
3 tablespoons of plain flour
A little oil for frying

What you do:
1. Put the cornflakes in a clean plastic bag and whack them until they are crushed, but not turned to dust. I like to think of Melissa while I'm whacking — Megan Pour the cornflake crumbs onto a big plate.
2. Beat the egg and milk together and pour onto another plate. Put the flour onto a third plate.
3. Roll each piece of fish in the flour, then in the egg and then in the cornflakes. Press the cornflakes onto the fish with your fingers, so they stick well.
4. Pour the oil into a frying pan and let it heat up for a minute or two. Then add the coated fish and let it cook over a medium heat for about 5 minutes on each side.

You can swap the fish for strips of chicken breast, but you'll need to cook them for a bit longer — Megan
Don't swap the cornflakes for coco pops — I did and it's gross! — Alice

Small & Spicy Fishcakes

These are lovely if you have something to dip them in. We like sweet chilli sauce best but you could also try ketchup or mayonnaise. Serve with salad, or noodles and stir-fried vegetables.

For four fishcakes you will need:

1 slice of white bread

About a half centimetre of fresh ginger, peeled and chopped

Half a red chilli (or more if you're very brave), washed and chopped with the seeds removed

3 cloves of garlic peeled and chopped

1 dessertspoon of lemon or lime juice

About a tablespoon of fresh coriander roughly chopped

Some salt and pepper

250g of skinless sustainable white fish.

1 egg

About a tablespoon of flour for coating.

A little oil for frying.

What you do:

1. Break up the bread and put it into a food processor.
2. Add the ginger, chilli, garlic, lemon or lime juice, coriander and salt and pepper.
3. Blitz in the food processor until everything is finely chopped.
4. Now cut your fish into chunks, add to the food processor and blitz again until you have an evenly chopped, stiff paste.
5. Unplug the food processor, and take the fish mix from the bowl. Use your hands to make the fish mix into small balls, then flatten into cake shapes.
6. Put the flour on a plate. Beat the egg and pour onto another plate.
7. Roll each cake in the flour, and then dip them into the egg.
8. Heat the oil in a large frying pan over a medium heat. When the oil is hot, add the fish cakes and cook for 5 minutes on each side.
9. Serve.

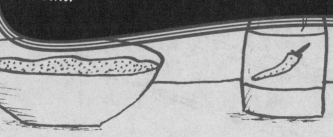

PEMBROKE BRANCH TEL. 6689575

Pasta & Tomato Sauce

These two go together like Megan and Bruno – Ha, ha!

For four people you will need:
4 portions of your favourite pasta
1 small onion
2 cloves of garlic
Half a red pepper
1 can of chopped tomatoes
Some fresh basil or a teaspoon of pesto (optional, but nice if you can get them)
A little black pepper
1 teaspoon of brown sugar
A little oil for frying

What you do:
1. Heat a little oil in a saucepan.
2. Peel and finely chop the onion, then peel and finely chop, or crush, the garlic. Wash and de-seed the pepper, and chop it finely.
3. Add the all of these ingredients to the pan, and cook for about five minutes, until soft, but not brown.
4. Add the tomatoes, a grind of black pepper and the sugar. Then add the basil or pesto (if using).
5. Bring to a simmer and allow to simmer for 15 minutes.
6. While the sauce is simmering, cook the pasta according to the packet instructions.
7. When the pasta is cooked, drain it and divide between four plates, and top with the sauce. You can grate over some cheese, and sprinkle with chopped parsley if you like.

Sweet & Sour Chicken

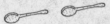

Mum never lets me get sweet and sour chicken in a take-away, but Alice says I shouldn't care as this version is much, much nicer. And much better for you too – Sheila

Always use a separate chopping board & knife for raw meat!

Serve this with rice or noodles.

For four people you will need:

4 boneless chicken breasts, chopped into small, evenly-sized pieces
5 cloves of garlic, peeled and crushed (or chopped finely)
3cm piece of fresh ginger, peeled and chopped finely
1 red pepper, washed, deseeded and chopped
2 sticks of celery washed and chopped
1 onion peeled and chopped
About 8 runner beans washed, trimmed and chopped
A little oil for frying

Sauce ingredients:

9 tablespoons of tomato ketchup
3 tablespoons of white wine vinegar
2 tablespoons of brown sugar
220g can of pineapple chunks in juice (not in syrup as the sauce will be too sweet)

Always make sure chicken is well cooked; there must be no pink at all left!

What you do:

1. Pour some oil into a wok or large frying pan, and put over a medium heat for a few minutes. When the oil is hot add the chicken and cook for ten minutes. (Cut the biggest piece and make sure that there is no trace of pink inside. If there is, cook for a few more minutes.)
2. Set the chicken aside, add some more oil to the pan, and cook the vegetables for 4-5 minutes, stirring all the time.
3. Mix all the sauce ingredients together in a bowl. Add the sauce to the pan, and add the cooked chicken. Stir everything together, and let it bubble for a few minutes.
4. Pour over your cooked rice or noodles.

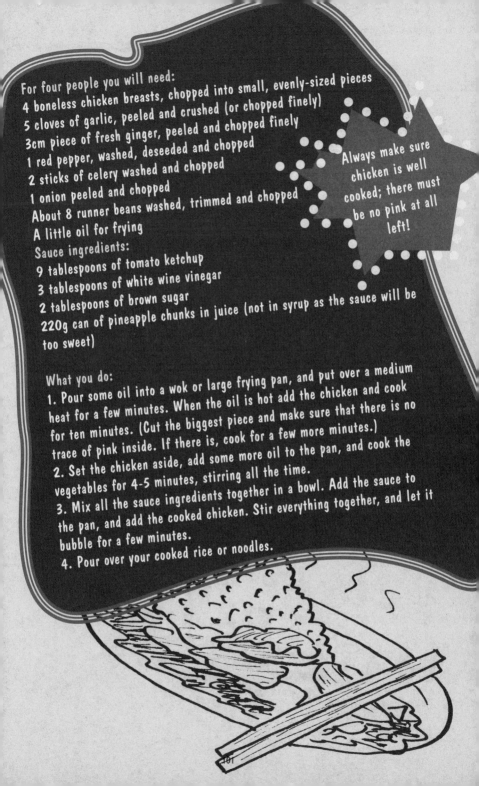

Fabulous Fajitas

We love these the way they are, but if you like, you can add some cooked chicken or beef to the cooked vegetables and stir-fry for a minute or two to warm up. Then serve with accompaniments as below.

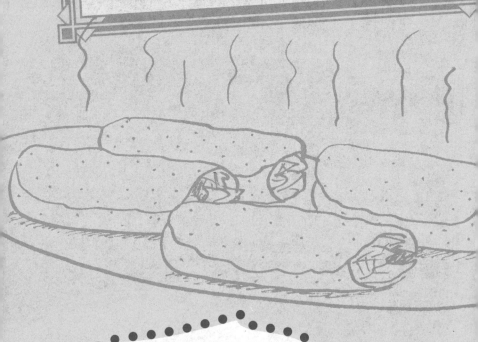

Accompaniments:
You can try any (or all) of these in fajitas: shredded lettuce, sprouted seeds, sweet chilli sauce, grated cheese, slices of red onion, crème fraiche.

For four people you will need:
1 red chilli
1 red (or yellow or orange) pepper
1 onion
4 tablespoons of sweetcorn (frozen, or from a can)
Juice of 1 lime (or lemon)
Half a teaspoon of paprika (optional)
A packet of tortilla wraps
A little oil for frying
Accompaniments (see below left)

What you do:
1. Wash the chilli, and slit it down the middle. Discard the seeds and the green top, and chop the rest into fine slivers.
2. Wash and de-seed the pepper, and cut into narrow strips.
3. Peel and finely chop the onion.
4. Take the sweetcorn out of the packet or can.
5. Heat the oil in a wok, or large frying pan, then add the vegetables to the wok.
6. Cook the vegetables for 4-5 minutes. Add the paprika. Squeeze in the lime (or lemon) juice and stir well.
7. Heat the wraps according to the packet instructions.
8. Serve the veg mix in a large serving dish, and put the warm wraps on a plate. Put your chosen accompaniments on the table. It's fun if you let everyone assemble their own wraps!

Tip
You can include other vegetables if you like — try green beans, mangetout or mushrooms.

Divine
Desserts

Cheesecakes in Glasses

We love cheesecake, but making it takes a while. These little cheesecakes are just as nice, but twice as quick. I wish Alice and I had known about these when we were making dinner for her dad and my Aunt Linda! (If we had, they might have forgiven us sooner.)

For six people you will need:
150g of blueberries
1 tablespoon of caster sugar
6 digestive biscuits
30g of butter
250g tub of mascarpone
The juice of 1 lemon
3 tablespoons of icing sugar

What you do:
1. Make sure you have six large, pretty glasses for serving the dessert.
2. Put the blueberries and caster sugar into a saucepan, and simmer for 3-4 minutes until the blueberries are just starting to burst. Set aside to cool.
3. Melt the butter (either in the microwave, or over a saucepan of boiling water). 'Tips & Techniques' p15.
4. Put the biscuits into a plastic bag and whack them until they are in crumbs.
5. Mix the biscuits and butter together, and spoon into the glasses. (Don't press it down as this would make it hard to eat later.)
6. Put the mascarpone into a bowl. Add the lemon juice and icing sugar and mix well.
7. Add the some of the blueberries to the glasses, and then some of the mascarpone mix. Continue to add blueberries and mascarpone mix to the glasses in alternating layers, finishing with mascarpone. Drizzle any remaining blueberry juice over the top.
8. Serve.

Tips
Try using ginger nut biscuits instead of digestives.
You can also try different types of berries. Blackberries work well — and you can pick your own in the autumn. Raspberries and strawberries are yummy, too. If you use strawberries, you don't need to cook them first and, as they are quite sweet, you can cut down on the sugar you add, too.

Baked Bananas

Lots of fruit is great baked – warm and juicy and totally delicious. Try these yummy baked bananas.

These are delicious as they are, but for a special treat, you could serve them with fresh cream or ice-cream.

For four servings you will need:

2 large bananas

The grated zest and juice of half an orange (save yourself heaps of trouble, and grate the zest before cutting the orange in half)

15g of butter

1 dessertspoon of brown sugar

A little oil or butter to grease the baking tray

What you do:

1. Preheat the oven to 200 degrees / gas 7.
2. Grease a shallow dish that will be big enough to hold the bananas when cut lengthways.
3. Peel the bananas and cut in half lengthways. Place in the dish, with cut sides facing up.
4. Sprinkle the orange rind, juice and sugar over the bananas, then dot with butter.
5. Put into the oven and leave to cook for 10-12 minutes, until soft, but not too brown.
6. Serve the bananas on plates with the warm juices sprinkled around them.

Tip

If you have a passion fruit lying around the kitchen, you could scrape the flesh onto the bananas before cooking.

Baked peaches or nectarines are also yummy — especially if you do them in summertime when they are lovely and juicy. Wash them, cut in half and remove the stones. Put on a baking tray, (cut side up) and sprinkle each side with a little brown sugar and a dribble of cream. Bake at 180 degrees / gas 5 for twenty minutes.

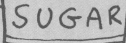

Eton Mess

This dessert got its name from a school in England called Eton. Eton is a very, very fancy school – even fancier than Melissa's boarding school. Every summer, since forever, they've had a big posh picnic, and all the mums and dads try their hardest to make the best picnic food. One year, one of the mums invented this dessert and called it 'Eton Mess.' You'll know why when you make it. (Actually, I bet the mum made a very fancy Pavlova, and then dropped it on the way to the picnic. Instead of owning up to being so clumsy, she pretended that it was meant to be all mixed up.)

For six people you will need:
(This isn't the kind of dessert that needs exact measurements, that's why I like it so much)
A punnet of fresh, juicy strawberries
2 teaspoons of caster sugar
A few meringues. If you are posh (like those Eton people), you can make your own using the recipe on page 120, but ones from a shop are fine.
A small carton of cream.

What you do:
1. Make sure you have six pretty glasses to serve the dessert.
2. Wash the strawberries and remove the green tops. Cut the strawberries into chunks and put them into a large bowl with two teaspoons of caster sugar. Stir.
3. Whip the cream until slightly thickened, and stir into the strawberries.
4. Now crumble in the meringues and stir again, gently.
5. Spoon the mixture into your pretty glasses and serve at once, before the meringues have time to go soft.

Tip
It's hard to improve on this, but you could try turning it into 'Banoffee Mess'. Just leave out the strawberries and sugar, and instead mix in two chopped bananas and a few tablespoons of caramel sauce from a jar.

Ice Cream & Toffee Sauce

Sugary liquids burn easily, so keep an eye on the heat under your saucepan. Burnt toffee sauce is gross!

Sugary liquids burn tongues, so resist the temptation to taste this while it's cooking!

ICE CREAM

What you will need:
50g of butter
50g of caster sugar
75g of brown sugar
125g of golden syrup
125ml of cream
Enough vanilla ice-cream for everyone

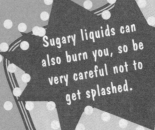

Sugary liquids can also burn you, so be very careful not to get splashed.

What you do:
1. Put all of the ingredients — except for the ice-cream — into a saucepan, and simmer over a medium heat for 5-6 minutes, stirring all the time. Leave to cool for five minutes.
2. Spoon some of the ice-cream into your prettiest glasses or bowls, and drizzle lots of the yummy warm sauce over the top.

Tips
Make this even yummier and healthier by adding some fruit to the bowls. Try bananas and strawberries.
If you have any sauce left — this has never happened us — put it in a jar in the fridge, and it will keep for ages.

Melting Chocolate Pots

For five small, or four slightly bigger, pots you will need:

125g of butter
100g of milk chocolate
3 (hens') eggs
150g of caster sugar
35g of plain flour
A little extra butter or oil for greasing

What you do:

1. Use the extra butter or oil to grease four or five small heatproof bowls (ramekins).
2. Preheat the oven to 200 degrees / gas 7.
3. Put the butter and chocolate into a bowl over a pan of simmering water. Stir occasionally until it is melted and blended. 'Tips & Techniques' p15.
4. Break the eggs into another bowl, and add the caster sugar and flour. Mix well with a whisk.
5. Very slowly, add the melted chocolate mixture to the egg mixture, mixing well all the time. (The bowl will be hot, so pick it up with oven gloves.) If you only have two hands ask a friend to help with this bit.
6. Pour the mixture into the greased heatproof bowls or ramekins.
7. Put the ramekins onto a flat baking sheet, and put the sheet into the oven for about 12-14 minutes. When they are done, the outsides and tops will be firm, but the middles will be totally delicious and gooey.

Note

You need to eat these as soon as they are cooked. If you like, you can prepare them before your dinner. You can pour the mixture into the ramekins and they will be fine for about 45 minutes before cooking.

Apple Crumble

Serve with custard, cream or ice-cream.

For one large crumble you will need:
200g of cold butter, cut into small chunks
100g of plain flour
100g of wholemeal flour
130g of brown sugar
75g of porridge oats (or sugar-free muesli)
750g of cooking apples
1 tablespoon of caster sugar
A little extra butter for greasing the pie dish

What you do:
1. Preheat the oven to 180 degrees / gas 6.
2. Put the chopped butter, flours, brown sugar and porridge oats (or muesli) into a large bowl. Rub together with your fingers until the mixture looks like large breadcrumbs. Set aside.
3. Peel and core the apples and chop into chunks
4. Butter a large ovenproof pie dish, place the apples in the bottom and sprinkle with the caster sugar.
5. Pour the crumble mix over the apples and bake for 30-40 minutes until the apples are soft and juicy and the crumble is golden brown.

Tips
Crumble works with all kinds of fruit, so you can use what you like or what you can get your hands on. Mixtures of fruit work too.
You could try: rhubarb, blueberries, blackberries, plums, a mixture of nectarines and strawberries, or a mixture of peaches and raspberries.
Wash all fruit before using. Chop big stuff like rhubarb and peaches.
Remove hard stones from peaches, plums and nectarines.
Sprinkle sugar over fruit depending on how sweet they are to start with.

Orange Sunsets

For six people you will need:
3 large oranges
One packet of orange jelly

What you do:
1. Cut the oranges in half, and squeeze out the juice. Use a spoon to scoop out the dry flesh of the orange, and discard. Keep the halved orange skins — you'll need them later.
2. Pour the juice into a measuring jug; the jelly packet will tell you how much juice you should have in the jug. Oranges (like people) are all different, so you might have too much or too little juice. If you have too little, you can add some hot water. If you have too much, just drink some — it's good for you.
3. Now put the jelly and the juice into a saucepan.
Take the jelly out of the packet first — Megan
4. Put the saucepan over a low heat and stir until jelly is dissolved.
5. Stand the orange halves on a muffin tray to stop them wobbling about. Pour the jelly and juice mixture back into the jug, and then into orange halves. Put them into the fridge to set for a few hours, or overnight. (If you have too much jelly, put the rest in a bowl for second helpings.)
6. When they're set, eat them straight from the oranges with a spoon.

Tip
If you want, you can add some extra fruit before pouring the jelly into the orange shells. You could try grapes, or segments of mandarin orange.

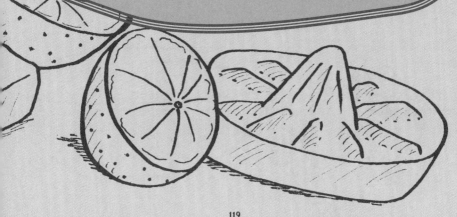

Raspberry Meringue Sandwiches

For about sixteen meringue sandwiches you will need:
2 egg whites
100g of caster sugar
About 150g of fresh raspberries
150ml of cream

What you do:
1. Grease 2 large baking sheets, and line with baking parchment.
Preheat the oven to 110 degrees / gas 1.
2. Put the egg-whites into a large clean bowl, and whisk until the mixture
stands up in stiff peaks.
3. Now add the caster sugar, a little at a time, whisking well each time.
When you are finished, the mixture should be thick and shiny.
4. Put teaspoon-sized blobs of the mixture onto your baking sheets. (Don't
put them too close together or they will stick together when cooking.)
5. Put into the oven and bake for one hour. Take the tray from the oven.
Carefully peel the meringues from the paper and put on a wire rack to cool.
6. Once the meringues are cool, wash the raspberries and whip the cream
until it's thick.
7. Spread cream on the flat side of a meringue, and gently squish a few
raspberries on top. Spread a little cream on the flat side of another
meringue, and gently sandwich them together.
8. Repeat with the rest of the meringues, and then arrange them on a pretty
plate. If you have raspberries left over, you can scatter them alongside. If
you run out of raspberries ... well, work it out so that doesn't happen!

Tips
If you mess up when separating the eggs and some of the yolk gets mixed in
with the white, I'm afraid you're going to have scrambled eggs for tea.
That's because even the tiniest scrap of yolk will stop the white from
whisking properly.
This dessert also works well using strawberries or sliced peaches instead
of raspberries.

Strawberry Mallow Surprise

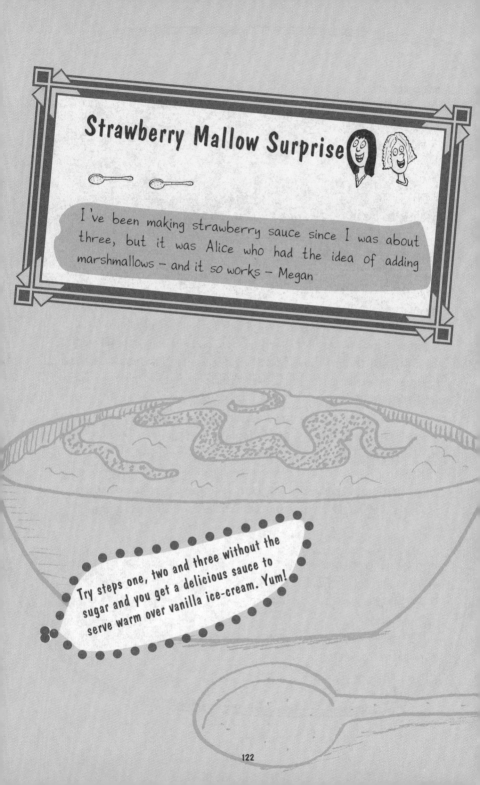

I've been making strawberry sauce since I was about three, but it was Alice who had the idea of adding marshmallows — and it so works — Megan

Try steps one, two and three without the sugar and you get a delicious sauce to serve warm over vanilla ice-cream. Yum!

For 4-6 people you will need:
250g of fresh strawberries
2 dessertspoons of caster sugar
100ml of cold water
150g of pink or white marshmallows
200ml of cream

What you do:
1. Cut the green tops off the strawberries. Put the strawberries into a saucepan with the caster sugar and the water. Simmer on a medium heat for five minutes until soft.
2. Remove the saucepan from the heat and mash the strawberries with a potato masher until turned to pulp. (If you are very fussy about squishy things, you could push them through a sieve.) Save a few dessertspoons of the mix in a small bowl for decoration.
3. Add the marshmallows to the pot of hot strawberries and stir until they have dissolved. Leave the mix to cool for about twenty minutes.
4. Whip the cream until fairly stiff, and then fold into the cooled strawberry mallow mix. Pour into six pretty bowls or glasses and put into fridge for an hour or two until set.
5. When the Strawberry Mallow Surprise is set, remove from fridge and swirl a spoon of the strawberry mix you kept for decoration on top.

Chocolate Cheesecake

This takes a while to make, but it looks very fancy – a good one for special occasions.

What you will need:

300g of bourbon cream biscuits
90g of butter
290ml of cream
225g of cottage cheese
225g of soft cheese (like Philadelphia)
50g of caster sugar
The juice of 1 lemon
3 tablespoons of boiling water
1 sachet of gelatine
35g of dark chocolate

What you do:

1. Take out a springform tin measuring 23-25 cm and your food processor.
2. Put the butter into a large saucepan and heat until melted.
3. Put the biscuits into the bowl of the food processor and whizz until finely crumbled.
4. Pour the biscuit crumbs into the melted butter and mix well. Pour the mixture into the springform tin, press down with a potato masher or the back of a spoon and put into the fridge to cool.
5. Break up the chocolate and put in a bowl over a pan of simmering water to melt, stirring occasionally.
6. While the chocolate is melting, rinse the food processor bowl, add the cheeses, cream, sugar and lemon juice and whizz until well blended.
7. Put three tablespoons of boiling water into a small bowl, sprinkle the gelatine over, and stir until it dissolves. (If the gelatine won't dissolve, put the bowl over a pan of simmering water and heat and stir again.)
8. Now add the gelatine and water to the cheese mix in the food processor, and whizz again.
9. Pour the mixture onto the biscuit base.
10. Immediately, spoon blobs of the melted chocolate on to the cheese mixture. Use a cocktail stick or a skewer to stir the chocolate over the surface making nice, swirly patterns — this is the fun bit!
11. Put the cheesecake into the fridge for 1-2 hours until the top has set.
12. When it is set, carefully remove the outside of the tin, and serve.

Cakes & Cookies

Chocolate Biscuit Cake

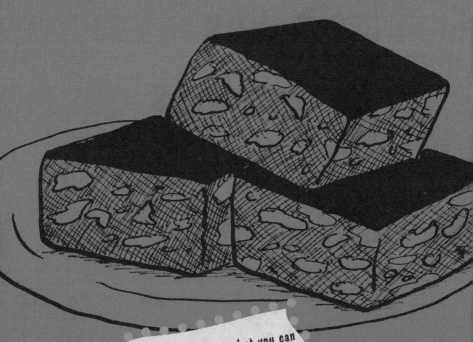

This is delicious as it is, but you can have fun with adding other stuff. Try adding some Smarties or mini marshmallows to the bashed-up biscuits. (Note to Sheila: Brussels sprouts don't work!)

For about sixteen slices you will need:
2 packets of Lincoln Biscuits
3 dessertspoons of golden syrup
2 tablespoons of drinking chocolate powder
115g of butter
A 100g bar of milk chocolate
A little butter for greasing

What you do:
1. Get out a 22cm square baking tin, grease it with a little butter and then line it with greaseproof paper. (Let the paper go up over the sides so that you can use it to lift out the cake later.)
2. Put the biscuits into a clean plastic bag, and bash with a rolling pin until well broken up, but not turned to dust. Pour the broken biscuits into a large bowl.
3. Put the golden syrup, the drinking chocolate powder and the butter into a saucepan. Heat it over a low heat on the cooker. Stir until melted and well mixed together.
4. Pour the syrup mix over the broken biscuits and stir well.
5. Pour the mixture into the prepared tin. Spread it well out into corners — you can use a potato masher to press it down well.
6. Put it into the fridge for half an hour to set.
7. Place the chocolate in a bowl, and then melt it over a saucepan of simmering water. See 'Tips & Techniques' p15.
8. Spread the melted chocolate over the biscuit cake.
9. Put the biscuit cake back into the fridge until chocolate is set. Then use the greaseproof paper to lift it from the tin. Put it on a flat surface, and cut into even-sized squares.

Sugary liquids can burn you, so be very careful not to get splashed.

Luscious Lemon Cupcakes

For twelve cupcakes you will need:
40g of softened butter
110g of plain flour
120g of caster sugar
1 and a half teaspoons baking powder
The finely grated zest of half a lemon
1 tablespoon of lemon juice
90ml of milk
1 medium egg

For the topping:
120g of icing sugar (sieve before using)
50g of softened butter
1 dessertspoon of lemon juice
The finely grated zest of half a lemon

What you do:
1. Take out a bun tray and twelve bun cases; put the bun cases into the tray. Take out your electric mixer / beater.
2. Preheat the oven to 170 degrees / gas 5.
3. Put the butter, flour, sugar, baking powder and lemon zest into a large bowl and mix well with the electric beater until you get a sandy kind of mixture.
4. Put the milk and egg into a small bowl and beat together, then pour about half of this mixture into the flour mixture and beat at high speed until it is smooth and lump-free.
5. Now add the rest of the milk mixture and the lemon juice, and mix at low speed, but don't mix too long at this stage, or your cakes won't be light!
6. Spoon the mixture into the bun cases and bake for 15-20 minutes. You'll know they're cooked if the tops bounce back when touched lightly with your finger. Carefully remove the cupcakes from the tin and put them on a wire tray to cool.
7. While the cakes are cooling, make the topping. Put all the ingredients into a bowl, and mix well with an electric mixer until fully blended and soft.
8. When the cakes are fully cooled, spread the icing on top and arrange them on your prettiest plate. Enjoy!
Tips
For special occasions, you could colour the topping by adding a drop of food colouring to the mixture.
Only do this if Jamie isn't around, and Sheila isn't looking — Alice
You could also decorate with coloured sprinkles, or even little shreds of lemon zest.

For about sixteen brownies you will need:

250g of butter chopped into cubes
160g of white chocolate
80g of dark chocolate
80g of milk chocolate
220g of golden caster sugar
4 eggs, beaten
150g of plain flour

What you do:
1. Grease and line a 24cm square brownie tin.
2. Preheat the oven to 160 degrees / gas 4.
3. Now you need two large heatproof bowls and two saucepans.
4. Put 125g of butter into each bowl. Then put the white chocolate into one bowl and the milk and dark chocolate into the other.
5. Melt each bowl of chocolate over a pan of simmering water. 'Tips & Techniques' p15. Stir until the butter and chocolates are melted and well-mixed together.
6. Remove the bowls from the heat. Add two beaten eggs and 110g of caster sugar to each bowl. Mix well.
7. Now add 75g of flour to each bowl and mix well again.
8. Now the fun starts! Spoon blobs of light and dark mix into the lined tin. When the base is covered, continue adding blobs, putting dark on light, and light on dark. Continue until the mixes are all used up (and don't worry if the two colours are mixing into each other a bit at the edges.)
9. Put into the oven and bake for 30-35 minutes, until the brownies are just about set.
10. Allow them to cool in the tin. When cool, remove from the tin and carefully peel off the lining paper. Put the cake onto a board and cut into chunks.
These are supposed to last for three or four days if you keep them in an airtight tin. We're not sure if that's true — they've never lasted for more than three or four hours in our houses!

Rosie's Favourite Chocolate Cake

For the cake you will need:
1 and a half tablespoons cocoa
4 tablespoons of hot water
200g of softened butter
200g of caster sugar
200g of self-raising flour
1 and a half teaspoons of baking powder
3 large eggs
3 tablespoons of milk

For the icing you will need:
75g of milk chocolate
3 tablespoons of water
25g of butter
3 tablespoons of icing sugar

Turn the page to see what to do!

What you do:

1. First, get a round tin measuring 22cm. Grease it, and line the bottom with a disc of greaseproof paper.
2. Switch on your oven to 180 degrees / gas 6.

That's the boring stuff over with, and now you can start to cook! – Alice

3. Measure the cocoa into a cup, add the hot water, and mix well.
4. Put the butter and sugar into a large mixing bowl. Beat very well with an electric hand beater (or with a wooden spoon if you are as strong as Alice!)
5. Sieve the flour and baking powder into a separate bowl.
6. Crack the first egg into a cup, and beat it lightly with a fork. Add it to the butter and sugar mixture with a dessertspoon of the flour/baking powder mix. Beat well.
7. Repeat this with the next two eggs.
8. Add the cocoa/hot water mix, and beat well.
9. Add the rest of the flour/baking powder mix, and fold in gently.
10. Add the milk and fold gently again.
11. Spoon into the baking tin, and smooth the surface.
12. Put the tin into the oven and bake for 35-40 minutes. You know it's done if you tap the top lightly, and it springs back.

13. When it's cooked, carefully run a knife around the edge of the cake to loosen it. Then turn the cake onto a wire tray, peel off the lining paper and leave the cake to cool.

Now make the icing:

1. Heat some water in a small saucepan.
2. Set a bowl over the saucepan, making sure the bottom isn't touching the water. 'Tips & Techniques' p 15
3. Into the bowl, put the chocolate, the 3 tablespoons of water, and the butter. Stir until everything is melted and mixed.
4. Sieve the icing sugar onto the chocolate mixture.
5. Stir until well mixed.
6. When the cake is fully cooled, spread the icing on top. Let some of the icing drip over the edges.
7. Find a safe place to hide the cake from Rosie so that the icing can set a little before eating!

Granny's Crunchy Biscuits

I always love it when my Granny visits, but when she brings a batch of these biscuits, she's more welcome than ever!

These biscuits won't win any beauty contests, but they are totally delicious. If things in your life absolutely have to be symmetrical and beautiful, just eat them with your eyes closed.

For 16-20 biscuits you will need:

170g of butter
110g of sugar
2 tablespoons of golden syrup
2 tablespoons of milk
170g of plain flour
170g of porridge oats
1 level teaspoon of bread soda
A little oil or butter for greasing the baking trays

What you do:

1. Put the butter, sugar, golden syrup, and milk into a large saucepan over a medium heat. Stir until the butter is melted and everything is mixed together.
2. Put the flour, porridge oats and bread soda into a large bowl and stir.
3. Add the butter, sugar, golden syrup and milk mixture and stir well.
4. Put the bowl into the fridge for half an hour to rest. (Not sure why flour and stuff needs to rest, but that's what Granny said.)
5. After half an hour, switch on your oven to 160 degrees / gas 4. Grease two large flat baking trays with oil or butter.
6. Make little teaspoon-sized balls of the mixture, and place on the trays. Flatten each one a little with a fork. Leave plenty of room between them as they spread out a lot.
7. Cook for 13-15 minutes until golden brown. Use a spatula to lift the biscuits from the trays to a wire rack. They may be a little wobbly when you take them out, but they will become firm as they cool.

Victoria Lemon Cake

Victoria was the queen of England, years and years ago. There are a few pictures of her in our history book, and she looks really cross in all of them. We don't know why that is because she had heaps of servants who made cakes for her every day. This kind of cake mix was her favourite, and that's why it's named after her.

For the cake you will need:
225g of softened butter
225g of caster sugar
The grated rind of one lemon
2 tablespoons of lemon juice
4 eggs
225g of self-raising flour
A little oil or butter for greasing the cake tins

For the butter icing (this goes in the middle):
75g of softened butter
150g of icing sugar, sieved
Grated rind of one lemon
1 tablespoonful of lemon juice

For the water icing (this goes on top):
175g of icing sugar sieved
5-6 teaspoons of lemon juice

Turn the page to see what to do!

What you do:
1. Grease two 20cm sandwich tins, and line with baking parchment.
2. Switch on your oven to 170 degrees / gas 5.
3. Put the butter, sugar and lemon rind into a bowl and beat with a wooden spoon or electric mixer until light and fluffy. (OK, so it takes ages if you use a wooden spoon, but the exercise is good for you!)
4. Add one egg and one tablespoon of flour and beat well.
5. Repeat with the other eggs, adding tablespoons of flour at the same time.
6. Now add the rest of the flour and fold it in. (That means stirring gently.)
7. Add the lemon juice and fold in.
8. Divide the mixture between the prepared tins, and smooth down with the back of a spoon. The cakes will rise (hopefully!), so if you want flat tops, try to make the centres of the cakes a tiny bit lower than the sides.
9. Put into the oven, and cook for about 25-30 minutes. Don't keep opening the oven to check, as the cakes will sink. When they're done, the tops will bounce back if you press them lightly with your fingers.
10. Take the cakes out of the tins, peel away the parchment and leave them on a wire rack to cool.

While the cakes are cooling, make the butter icing:

1. Put the butter, sugar, lemon rind and juice into a bowl and beat with a wooden spoon or an electric mixer until well-mixed and soft.
2. Spread this onto the top of one of your cooled cakes, then place the other cake on top.

Then make the water icing:

1. Stir the lemon juice and icing sugar together and spread this on top of your cake.
2. As soon as the icing has set, your cake is ready to eat.

Tips

Another reason Queen Victoria should have been happy is that you can do so many different things with this cake.
Instead of making icing and butter icing, you could try sandwiching the cake together with your favourite jam (or lemon curd) and some whipped cream. Then sieve a little bit of icing sugar over the top.
Or you could try leaving out the lemon in the cake and icings, and then you can do any of the following:

1. Make coffee cake: add two tablespoons of very strong coffee to the cake mix, after adding the flour. Add 1 tablespoonful of very strong coffee to the butter icing, and make the water icing with a tablespoon of coffee instead of the lemon juice.
2. Make orange cake, using orange rind and juice instead of lemon, in the cake mixture, and the icings.
(And if none of that brought a smile to Victoria's face, then nothing would have!)

Megan's Best-Ever Ice-Cream Birthday Cake

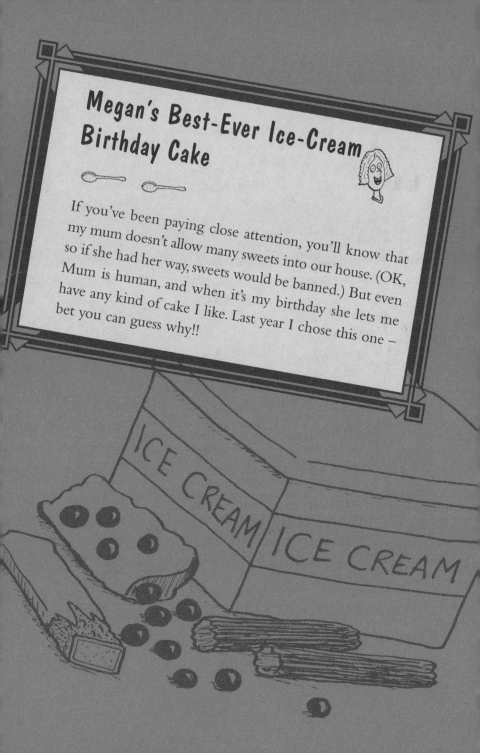

If you've been paying close attention, you'll know that my mum doesn't allow many sweets into our house. (OK, so if she had her way, sweets would be banned.) But even Mum is human, and when it's my birthday she lets me have any kind of cake I like. Last year I chose this one – bet you can guess why!!

For one big and totally yummy cake, you will need:
2 litres of vanilla ice-cream
150g of your favourite chocolate biscuits (I like chocolate digestives or Oreos)
1 chocolate Flake bar
Now for the fun bit — you also need 150g of your favourite sweet stuff —
anything small or that can be crushed into small pieces. (Hard sweets are not
suitable for this.) I like a combination of Crunchies, Maltesers, Toffee Crisp and
mini-marshmallows.

What you do:
1. Leave the ice-cream out of the freezer until it is soft enough to stir,
but isn't runny.
2. Hide the Flake.
3. Line a 26cm springform tin (that's the kind you use for cheesecakes) with
cling-film, leaving some hanging over the edges. You'll need the hanging-over
bits to cover the cake later. Don't worry too much about getting the cling-film
smooth, just make sure all the tin is covered or you will be really sorry later!
4. Put all the sweets except the Flake into a clean plastic bag and bash with a
rolling pin until they are in big crumbs. Pour the smashed sweets into a big
mixing bowl.
5. Use the same bag to crush the chocolate biscuits. Add to the sweets in the
bowl.
6. Now add the softened ice-cream to the bowl of bashed up stuff. Stir well, and
then pour it into the prepared cake tin. Smooth the top as much as you can, pull
the overhanging cling-film over the top to protect it. Put into the freezer for at
least two hours.
7. When you are ready to serve the cake, remember where you hid the Flake and
go and get it. If you hid it too well, and can't find it, or not well enough and
your little sister found it and ate it, go down to the shop and buy another one.
8. Take the cake out of the freezer, and remove it from the tin, using the cling-
film to help you. Carefully peel off the cling film. Put the cake onto a nice
serving plate. Use your (clean!) fingers to crumble the Flake over the top of the
cake, spreading it out as evenly as you can.
9. After about five minutes, the cake will be soft enough to cut into slices.
Eat before it melts!

Swirly Chocolate Cupcakes

Pretty and delicious!

For twelve cupcakes you will need:
15g of cocoa powder
100g of plain flour
130g of caster sugar
1 and a half teaspoons baking powder
A tiny pinch of salt
40g of softened butter
120 ml of milk
1 egg
For the topping:
75g of milk chocolate and 25g of white chocolate for topping

What you do:
1. Take out a bun tray and twelve bun cases; put the bun cases into the tray. Take out your electric mixer / beater.
2. Preheat the oven to 170 degrees / gas 5.
3. Put the cocoa powder, flour, sugar, baking powder, salt and butter into a large mixing bowl, and use an electric mixer to beat until everything is well mixed and looks a bit like sand.
4. Put the milk and egg into a small bowl and beat together. Pour about half of this mixture into the flour mixture and beat at high speed until it is smooth and lump-free.
5. Now add the rest of the milk mixture and mix at low speed (don't mix too long at this stage, or your cakes will be hard, and not very nice.)
6. Spoon the mixture into the bun cases, and bake for 15-20 minutes. You know they are cooked if the tops bounce back when touched lightly with your finger. When cooked, carefully remove from the tins, and put on a wire tray to cool.
7. When the cupcakes are fully cooled, break the two types of chocolate into two small bowls and melt them over two saucepans of simmering water. 'Tips & Techniques' p15.
8. Stir until the chocolate is melted, then spread the milk chocolate over the tops of the cupcakes. Immediately, spoon small drops of the white chocolate on top, and use a skewer or cocktail stick to swirl into pretty patterns.
The cupcakes are ready to eat as soon as the chocolate has set (if you can wait that long!)

Very Vanilla Cookies

I love these biscuits – they remind me of the biscuits my mother makes back home in Latvia – Luka

To make lots and lots of cookies you will need:

120ml of sunflower oil
125g of softened butter
60g of icing sugar
90g of caster sugar
1 egg
2 teaspoons of vanilla extract
250g of plain flour
Half a teaspoon of bread-soda
Quarter of a teaspoon of salt
A little oil for greasing

What you do:

1. Take out four large baking sheets and grease them very thoroughly with butter or oil.
2. Put the butter into a large bowl and beat with an electric mixer until soft. Now add the sunflower oil and beat well. (You'll discover that oil and butter don't always mix perfectly, but don't worry about that.)
3. Add the sugars, the egg and the vanilla extract and beat until well mixed.
4. Add the flour, bread soda and salt and mix briefly.
5. Cover the bowl and put it into the fridge for one hour. (Do your homework or text your friends or pick fights with your brothers and sisters while you are waiting.)
6. After an hour, pre-heat your oven to 180 degrees / gas 6.
7. Spoon dessertspoon-sized blobs of the mixture onto the greased baking sheets, and press them down lightly with your fingers. Leave lots of space around each one, as they will spread out a lot when cooking.
8. Cook for 8-10 minutes. Allow the cookies to cool on the tray for 5 minutes and then carefully use a spatula to lift them onto a wire rack to finish cooling.
9. These should keep for 3-4 days in an airtight container, but we've never managed to find out for sure!

Tips

This mixture makes loads of cookies, so if you're not expecting friends around, you could wrap half the mixture up in clingfilm to freeze and use another time. Just defrost when you want it and cook as above.
You could also make giant cookies by making bigger blobs. These will take a minute or two longer to cook.

Brown Bread

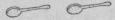

Ok, so bread isn't the most exciting thing in the world, but when you make it yourself and it's delicious and warm and fresh from the oven there's nothing like it, so go ahead and try it!

For one loaf you will need:

300g of coarse-ground wholemeal flour
150g of plain white flour
Half a teaspoon of salt
1 teaspoon of bread soda
50g of butter
300ml of buttermilk
1 egg
A little bit of butter for greasing the loaf tin

What you do:

1. Get out a loaf tin measuring about 10cm by 23cm.
2. Grease the loaf tin with a little bit of butter.
3. Heat your oven to 220 degrees / gas 9.
4. Put all the dry ingredients — the two types of flour, the salt and the bread soda — into a large mixing bowl and stir well.
5. Cut the butter into small cubes, and then rub them into the flour mix. Keep rubbing the butter and the dry ingredients between your fingers until the mixture looks like fine breadcrumbs.
6. Measure the 300ml of buttermilk in a large measuring jug. Beat the egg in a cup, and then mix it into the buttermilk.
7. Pour the buttermilk and egg mix into the flour mix and stir well.
8. Put the mixture into the greased loaf tin and smooth the top. Run a knife along the middle of the tin lengthways, making a shallow line in the top of the bread.
9. Put into the oven and cook for 15 minutes, then lower the heat to 200 degrees / gas 7 and cook for another 20 minutes. Take the bread out of the tin and tap the bottom. If it sounds hollow, it's cooked. If not, leave it upside down in the tin, and cook for another five minutes.
10. Cool on a wire rack. This bread is yummiest when it's just cool enough to cut without crumbling, but still slightly warm in the centre.

Temperature Conversions

	Electricity °C	Electricity (fan) °C	Gas Mark
Very cool	110	90	¼
	120	100	½
Cool	140	120	1
	150	130	2
Moderate	160	140	3
	180	160	4
Moderately hot	190	170	5
	200	180	6
Hot	220	200	7
	230	210	8
Very hot	240	220	9

Best friends
NEED to be
together.
Don't they?

Poor Megan! Not only is she stuck with totally uncool
parents, and a little sister who is too cute for words, but
now her best friend, Alice, has moved away. Now Megan has
to go to school and face the dreaded Melissa all on her own.
The two friends hatch a risky plot to get back together.
But can their secret plan work?

It's mid-term break and Megan's off to visit Alice.

Megan is hoping for a nice trouble-free few days with her best friend. No such luck! She soon discovers that Alice is once again plotting and scheming. It seems that Alice's mum, Veronica, has a new boyfriend. The plan is to discover who he is, and to get rid of him!

Alice and Megan are together again!

They are both looking forward to their Confirmation, especially as their two families are going out to dinner together to celebrate. But not even a meal can be simple when Alice is around as she decides to hatch a plan to get her parents back together ...

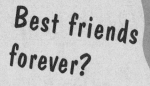

Best friends forever?

Megan can't wait to go away to Summer Camp with Alice! It will be fantastic — no organic porridge, no school, nothing but fun! But when Alice makes friends with Hazel, Megan begins to feel left out. Hazel's pretty, sophisticated and popular, and Alice seems to think she's amazing.

Is Megan going to lose her very best friend?

Sunshine & yummy French food — sounds like the perfect holiday!

Megan's really looking forward to the summer holidays — her whole family is going to France, and best of all Alice is coming too! But when Alice tries to make friends with a local French boy things begin to get very interesting …

Alice and Megan are starting secondary school.

New subjects, new teachers and new friends — it's going to take a bit of getting used to. And when Megan meets Marcus, the class bad-boy who's always in trouble (but doesn't seem to care) things really start to get complicated. At least she has Home Ec class with Alice — the worst cook in the school — to look forward to, so school's not all bad!

Winning is a good thing, isn't it?

Everyone in first year is really excited about the big prize in the English essay competition — four months in France!

Megan loves writing essays, but she doesn't want to win — go away for four months alone, no way! She doesn't want Alice to go either — why would anyone want to go abroad without her best friend? But Alice seems determined to get the prize...

WHY NOT VISIT THE GREAT NEW 'ALICE & MEGAN' WEBSITE AT
www.aliceandmegan.com